Dark Isle

Written by David Longhorn
Edited by Emma Salam

ISBN-13: 978-1540391902
ISBN-10: 1540391906

Thank You!

Hi there! I'd like to take this opportunity to thank you for purchasing this book. I really appreciate it, and to show how grateful I am to you I'd like to give you a bonus full length novel absolutely FREE.

Sign up for our mailing list below and receive Sherman's Library Trilogy by Ron Ripley, which offers many thrills and chills!
www.ScareStreet.com/DavidLonghorn

Yours eerily,
David Longhorn

Prologue: England, July 1916

Professor Montague Summerskill finished his pint of cider, and dabbed at his mouth with a napkin. He bade a cheery farewell to the landlord who was collecting glasses from the tables outside the village inn. The landlord nodded politely, but Summerskill wondered if he detected a glint of amusement in the stout countryman's eye.

Well, one can hardly blame him. The sight of a gentleman, no longer young and agile, clambering onto a bicycle is often somewhat ridiculous. He is anticipating a cabaret of sorts!

Trying to dispel such thoughts, Summerskill put on his cloth cap then wheeled his heavy, iron-framed bicycle away from the wall of the pub and into the country lane. He decided to go on foot a little further, until he was shielded from any onlookers at the pub or in the village by the tall hedgerows. As he walked on, the midday-sun beat down upon his tweed-clad form. He realized, not for the first time, that he was over-dressed for his little holiday.

Ah, well, proprieties must be observed! One can hardly go around in shirtsleeves!

Summerskill decided that he was far enough from mocking eyes to mount up, but then realized that he was going uphill. He decided to push his machine to the crest of the gentle rise, then freewheel down the other side. The prospect of such a simple, boyish pleasure coupled with a good pub lunch and some cider buoyed up his spirits. He was feeling much more confident, far happier than he had been for months. A great burden seemed to have been lifted from his shoulders.

I was silly to be so afraid, Summerskill thought. *A few strange incidents, a bizarre coincidence or two, and I reacted like a superstitious peasant. Or a scared child. After all, this is 1916, not the Middle Ages!*

A gust of wind blew down the hill, stirred the hedgerows, and ruffled his thinning hair. It should have been welcoming, cooling in the heat of the summer afternoon. But it brought no relief to Summerskill. It was a surprisingly hot wind, even for such a warm day.

Well, he thought, *when I'm freewheeling down the hill, I'll generate my own refreshing breeze.*

He reached the top of the rise and looked down the country lane that wound through the wheat fields of Cambridgeshire. Below him was a small farm, consisting of a quaint cottage, some neat outbuildings, and a small duck-pond. It was a picture of rural serenity, a vista unchanged for centuries. Summerskill stood for a minute enjoying the view. *All this fine weather bodes well for the harvest,* he reflected. But that led him to reflect on the terrible harvest of young lives in France.

Of course, German barbarism had to be opposed. But after nearly two years of war, Summerskill hadn't gotten used to reading out the names of his former students in the college chapel, leading the prayers for those who made the ultimate sacrifice. What was worse, the faces of the dead that had haunted his dreams for weeks.

So many young faces, he thought. *And here I am, a silly old fool enjoying a cycling holiday. Attempting to clear my mind of what can only be an absurd psychological fixation.*

Montague Summerskill had been ordered to go on holiday by his doctor, who also happened to be an old friend. The medic had told him that overwork combined with distressing war news had led to the professor's 'morbid fantasies'.

"Get out in the fresh air and sunlight!" the doctor had ordered. "See the English countryside at its best this July, then come back to Cambridge refreshed and ready for teaching, able to inspire a new generation of young minds! You've spent far too much time dwelling on those absurd stories of yours. All that horror and spookery is bound to undermine a man's grasp of reality."

For the last eight days, the doctor's advice had been vindicated. Summerskill had gradually regained lost sleep, thanks in part to the strenuous exercise of cycling along winding country lanes. He had visited historic churches and museums, chatted with garrulous locals, and enjoyed simple rural fare at mealtimes. He had come to believe that the fear that had possessed him during the winter months had indeed been illusory.

Again, the gust of hot air came, this time stronger. It hit him in the face, dislodging his cap and almost knocking his eyeglasses askew. Summerskill bent down to try and retrieve his headgear, but another gust blew it away into a hedge.

"Dash it all!" exclaimed the professor, laying the bicycle on the grass verge. He retrieved his cap and was about to pick his bike up again when he felt an all-too-familiar sensation. It was a tingling in the center of his back.

No, no not again, he thought, trying to quell rising panic. *It's just in my mind, the product of a 'morbid imagination'.*

But he didn't look round. Instead he clambered onto his bike and pushed off, freewheeling down the hill. Another gust of wind came, this one even stronger than the last, and almost threw him off balance. He struggled to retain control of the heavy machine, succeeded, then hit a pothole in the country road and found himself hurtling through the air. He landed awkwardly, breaking his fall with his hands and ending up with badly skinned palms.

Terribly winded, Summerskill struggled to his feet, this time looking around in outright terror. There was no one in sight, but it was not a person he was afraid of, or at least, not exactly. He saw it, then, a dark patch moving through the nearest field in a great arc. Something was pressing the wheat down, something more substantial than any gust of wind yet no more visible. It was coming back toward him in a great curving arc.

The Follower is real! It always was real!

"Oh God, help me!" he gasped to himself, trying to heave the bicycle upright. But he was far too slow, and the invisible assailant crashed through the hedge and struck him again with a blast of furnace-hot air. He flailed his arms, fell backwards, again landing heavily. He felt a stab of agony as his wrist gave a sickening snap. The pain was almost as bad as the fear.

Summerskill managed to get back onto the bicycle and headed downhill, pedaling this time, trying to steer despite his fractured wrist. He glanced around, and saw the Follower sweeping towards him again. Branches crashed, leaves flew through the air, and then the thing was through the hedgerow and swirling around him. The burning hot vortex flung him sideways, but this time he avoided a fall and continued to pedal.

Instinct told him to make for the pond.

A thing of air and heat. My only chance.

As if it was aware of his intention, the Follower swung around in a tighter arc and hit him again. He almost fell off, recovered, then let out a howl of despair. Summerskill realized that his voice was more like that of a hunted animal than a renowned scholar.

***

Martha Grundy was busy teaching her daughter Ruby how to knead dough for bread when Star, their border collie, began making a fuss. Martha left the kitchen table for a moment and went to look out of the cottage door, which stood open to the fine July day.

"What's that daft animal about now?" asked Martha, cleaning her hands on her apron. Ruby, with a six-year-old's healthy curiosity, followed her mother outside. The woman and child emerged from the cottage just in time to see a man in brown riding his bicycle straight through the hedge by the duck-pond. The cyclist wobbled for a split-second, then fell off.

"Oh, my Lord!" exclaimed Martha, and set off across the farmyard to try and help the poor gentleman up. *Them bicycles is dangerous things,* she thought. *Almost as bad as motor cars.*

Star had similar ideas. The young dog went rushing up to the man, barking with excitement, tail wagging. Then the dog stopped, headed to one side, and gave a whine.

"Get away, get away!" shouted the man, waving his arms as he struggled to rise.

"Come away, now, Star!" called Martha, slightly annoyed at the gentleman's attitude. He had, after all, ridden his bicycle onto someone else's land. And it wasn't as if Star was a vicious dog. Far from it, the silly creature wanted to be friends and play with anyone who passed by.

"He won't hurt you, mister!" added Ruby helpfully, skipping happily along after her mother. This was much more fun than learning to bake.

Then something odd happened. The dog seemed to look past the man, started barking more ferociously now, giving way to fear. Then Star turned and fled around the side of a chicken coop.

"What's wrong with the blessed animal now?"

Martha, still wiping her floury hands on her apron, hesitated. There was something not quite right, here. It was no simple accident. The cyclist stood staring at her open-mouthed, as if in horror. Then, looking around him, he rushed diagonally across the farm yard and hurled himself into the pond. A great torrent of greenish water erupted as the man went full-length. Half a dozen ducks flapped in all directions, quacking in outrage.

The man stood up spluttering, strands of pond-weed dangling from his head and clothing. Martha stood looking at him, thinking he looked like a statue with strands of green weed dripping from his clothes. Then she began to laugh, at first covering her mouth in embarrassment, then doubled up in near-hysterics. Ruby joined in.

"Madam, you are in grave danger! Go back inside, I beg you!"

There was something about the man's tone and the way he began waving her away again that made Martha stop laughing. She straightened up, and as she did so she felt a blast of blistering hot air on her face.

The man turned and waded quickly away from Martha and Ruby, then climbed out of the pond on the wheat-field opposite the cottage. Just as he reached dry land there was a bubbling surge behind. The greenish pond-water heaved, bulged, and a man-like shape reared up six, seven, eight feet high. It towered over the stranger, who began to run again, crashing into the wheat.

Martha reached down and clutched her child.

"Keep away!" shouted Summerskill, as he stumbled through the field. The green figure emerged from the pond, glistening. It had long, heavy forelimbs and started to lope after Summerskill like an ape.

"Get back inside, Ruby!" shouted the woman, pushing her daughter towards the cottage.

"What was that thing, Mummy?" asked Ruby, eyes wide.

"I don't know, girl, you just get back indoors!" said her mother in her special no-nonsense voice.

Once they were back inside Martha started to close the door, intending to bolt and bar it. Then she changed her mind and after ordering Ruby to go upstairs and hide under her bed, Martha reached behind the door for her husband's old twelve-bore shotgun.

***

The professor knew he was losing ground. He could hear his pursuer crashing through the wheat, the sound of the huge being getting louder. All the terror he had tried to banish returned, multiplied by a thousand folds.

I can't escape, Summerskill thought in despair. *I never could. I was doomed from the very start. But at least I'm leading it away from innocent bystanders.*

He could hear the Follower laughing now; a breathless inhumane sound, deep and cruel. A huge hand grabbed him by the ankle and pulled him down. Winded, he tried to struggle onto his hands and knees, but a prodigious weight bore him down. He felt cold slime, stinking of rank pond-water, start to cover his head. His nose and mouth filled with the stinking ooze, and he tossed his head trying to dislodge the filth from his airways.

Darkness closed in. The last thing Montague Summerskill heard was a boom, not unlike distant thunder on a summer's evening.

***

"And you say you shot at this mysterious assailant, Mrs. Grundy?" asked the county coroner.

"I did not say that!" replied Martha Grundy, her voice shaking with nervousness. She had never given evidence before, and didn't like standing in front of a room full of strangers in her Sunday best clothes. She was doing her best to 'speak properly', that is, in the manner of the upper-classes. But that meant shunning her native dialect, and it threw her off her stride.

"I said as how I shot it, your honor! I put both barrels into it!"

There was a ripple of conversation among the onlookers, and the coroner rapped his gavel before turning to Martha again.

"You say it, Mrs. Grundy? Not 'him'?"

Martha took a deep breath then said, "It weren't no proper human person!"

This time it took three raps of the gavel to restore order.

"Indeed," said the coroner. "Which might explain why, when the police officer arrived, he found no evidence of any other person at the scene of the incident, just the body of Mister Summerskill?"

Martha shook her head emphatically.

"There was something there all right! I don't know if it was a person, but I shot it and it all fell apart, like, as if it were just made o' water out of the pond."

This time the laughter in the small courtroom was unrestrained and it took the coroner nearly a minute to achieve quiet.

"I will not hesitate to clear the court if this improper behavior continues!" he warned, looking pointedly at the jury, most of whom had joined in the merriment. Turning back to Martha he said, "Thank you, Mrs. Grundy, you may step down. Call Constable Naismith!"

The policeman was far less nervous than the farmer's wife. But it soon became evident that he too, was not entirely sure of his facts.

"Did you see any evidence of the assailant Mrs. Grundy claims she shot at?" asked the coroner.

"No, sir," replied Naismith. "But I did check the twelve-bore, and it had been fired."

The policeman seemed about to continue, but paused.

"Well, go on!" urged the coroner.

"I found the pellets, your honor. They were lying around the body of the deceased gentleman."

"Lying around him?"

"Yes," replied Naismith. "Some of them were on top of his body and fell off when I turned him over to check if he was alive."

"You mean the shotgun pellets had struck the deceased?" asked the coroner.

"No, sir!" insisted Naismith. "I mean they were lying on and around him. As if they'd hit something and then ...""

The policeman made a vague gesture, as if trying to describe something unimaginable, then gave up.

"They were lying around the body, your honor," he concluded with a sigh.

The next witness was the medical examiner, a doctor who testified that the cause of death was 'suffocation due to the inhalation of more than a quart of pond-water'.

"Did you find any evidence that Mister Summerskill was the victim of an assault?"

The doctor hesitated, then looked the coroner in the eye and said, "No, sir, there is not. But this is the first time I've known an able-bodied man to inhale a lungful of water, then climb out of a pond and run twenty yards across a field before dropping dead."

The gavel was put to more use, then the coroner dismissed the medical expert and tried to sum up the evidence for the jury. He also spelled out the range of verdicts that they were permitted to give under the English law. It took the jurors a good six hours of wrangling to finally reach a conclusion, and when it was announced the verdict was so archaic and unusual that even the national press noticed it.

'Death by the Visitation of God.'

When she heard, Martha Grundy gave a derisive snort.

"The Good Lord had nothing to do with it!"

And that was the last time she spoke of the matter.

Chapter 1: Publish or Perish

Mark Stine loved to walk in Cambridge in the first light of a summer morning, when the ancient city was just coming to life. He got up just before six and, after a shave and a shower, left his cramped single-bed apartment in St Caedmon's College then strolled out onto streets that were almost deserted. The air was cool and fresh, the June sun was just breasting the rooftops, and Mark had the town almost to himself.

Say what you like about the Brits, he thought, as he passed the beautiful 15th century college chapel, *when they get something right, they really get it right.*

He walked through the midtown area, taking his time, knowing it was still ten minutes until his favorite cafe opened. He took the opportunity to check his phone again, but there were no new messages since he'd gotten up. Then one popped up, an email from an unfamiliar address. He dabbed at the screen to open it, but got an error message instead. He frowned, tried again. This time the message opened. All the email contained was a link. Mark hesitated, his thumb hovering over the screen. Then he deleted the email.

Fallen for that one before and got some nasty malware, he thought. *Fool me once, shame on you. Fool me twice, shame on me.*

"Excuse me, sir, could you spare some change?"

He had been staring at his phone while walking, something he hated other people doing. He looked up to see that he had almost walked into a short, slender young woman. She looked tired, pale, her clothes worn and ill-matched. And she was wearing too many layers for a summer morning in southern England.

"Some change, sir? Please. If I have three quid I can get a coffee in McDonald's."

Mark glanced into a shop doorway to his left. Sure enough, there was an old sleeping bag heaped up there.

How can a town like Cambridge have people sleeping rough?

It was one of the many baffling things about this country,

the way in which wonderful architecture and great learning could exist alongside Victorian-style deprivation. He shrugged. He couldn't expect to understand this country after living here for just a year.

And it's not as if America is some kind of Utopia.

"Sure," he said, reaching into his jeans pocket. "Look, I've only got a ten pound note, take this."

"Oh, thanks," replied the young woman, giving a wan smile. "That's really kind of you."

"No problem, enjoy your coffee!" he said, trying to sound friendly but realizing he might just come across as a jerk. He walked on, feeling awkward and slightly depressed. The encounter had robbed the morning of its beauty.

He put his phone away and picked up his pace, weaving through the complex, and narrow streets of the ancient city. A good breakfast would perk him up. After all, he had a meeting to prepare for.

***

After thanking the good-looking American, Lucy shoved the ten pound note into her jacket and set off for Mickey-Ds, happy that she would be able to get a breakfast bagel as well as a good-sized coffee. She struggled to focus, as usual, on the task ahead. Lucy's mind tended to drift. At nineteen, she'd had several lifetimes' worth of woes thanks to a nightmare family and spells in hostels that were dangerous, violent places. Drugs and booze had taken their toll. She had trouble with words, found it difficult to grasp ideas sometimes. She had been clean for months now, but it wasn't easy because in a town full of students, she kept running into people who were selling all sorts of stuff. Even now she sometimes saw things that weren't there.

The man on the bicycle was a good example.

Lucy had her head down, staring at the sidewalk as she scuttled along, and didn't pay attention to the cyclist at first. But the creaking and clanking of the bike sounded so wrong, different from the near-silence of well-oiled ones ridden by thousands of locals, that Lucy glanced up.

The bike was weird and clunky, but the man riding it in a strange 'sit up and beg' posture was even odder-looking. He was wearing thick, old-fashioned clothes that must have been really hot even on a cool day. On his head he wore a cloth cap, the sort her granddad had called 'a cheese-cutter' thanks to its flat peak. As he pedaled, his bicycle chain rattled, the sound echoing in the narrow street.

Maybe they're making a film about the old days, she thought, and looked around for a camera crew. Cambridge was a popular location for television and movie makers, not to mention students on various media courses. But Lucy could see no sign of anyone but a team of bin men collecting the trash of one of the city's many restaurants. She looked round for the cyclist, but he was gone.

Focus, girl, she told herself. *Weird, yeah, but it's none of your business.*

***

After a leisurely breakfast, Mark walked over the broad swathe of parkland known for quaint medieval reasons, as Christ's Pieces, then crossed over the road onto Midsummer Common on his way to the River Cam. It was just after eight and Cambridge was coming to life. Dog-walkers were out in force, and cyclists were buzzing back and forth. The noise of traffic from the major highways was now perceptible; a background roar.

Mark took out his phone again and frowned. Another mystery email had appeared. He deleted it without thinking. Then there was one from Sue, his long-distance girlfriend, and he hesitated before deciding not to open it. Things had been a little fraught lately with Sue pointedly asking him whether he was coming back to the States as planned. He didn't want to, but hadn't come right out and asked her to come and join him in Britain. She had her own career, after all, and wouldn't take kindly to the notion of the 'loyal little woman' thing and dropping everything to stand by her man.

But I love it here, he thought, looking around at what the locals called the 'common'- as in common land. It was a great expanse of open grassland dotted with trees, crisscrossed by cycle paths, and with plenty of benches and picnic spots. It gave onto the Cam, which meandered slowly through the heart of the town. It wasn't hard to fall in love with a place full of beautiful buildings and fascinating people, surrounded by beautiful countryside, and just an hour from all the attractions of London.

So he had often thought; the hard part would be getting Sue to agree.

His relationship with Sue was complicated, mostly because of her folks. Mark had grown up in a chaotic home thanks to an alcoholic mother and a succession of 'uncles' she had brought home. Sue's family was, in theory, just what he had always wanted, close-knit and traditional. Unfortunately, he had discovered that, in practice, they were so close-knit and traditional that he could only stand to be in the same room with them for a couple of hours, tops.

When Sue had proudly told her parents that Mark was going to be a visiting professor in Cambridge for a year, her Dad had nearly exploded.

"What do you want to go to Europe for?" he had demanded. "Place is full of commies, fags, and ragheads!"

"Don't forget the Queen," Mark had replied, trying to make light of it.

But it was the thought of spending the rest of his life in the bosom of Sue's family that made him yearn for another year in England.

Mark was so trapped up in his thoughts that he didn't see the creature until the last second. He was walking in the shade of some oak trees when he came across it. Off to one side of the path was what he took to be a modernist sculpture. It looked like an oddly shaped mass of brownish wood, a rounded, lumpish form, vaguely oval at the top, about three feet wide, with two legs vanishing into the abundant grass.

Sculpture trail, maybe, he thought. Cambridge was always lively when it came to the arts, and there was always some new project on the go. His eyes adjusted to the gloom and he realized that some kind of rope was dangling from the top of the object, which stood about five feet high. To his horror, the rope suddenly jerked and swung to one side, swatting at the air with a kind of brush. Mark froze, staring in shocked incomprehension. It was a bizarre tentacle, part of a larger organism that was now emitting a snorting noise. A great head appeared in the gloom. Two brown eyes regarded him coolly, but Mark was much more impressed by its two curved horns that ended in wicked points.

It's a bull! I'm looking at a bull's backside! Maybe it's escaped from a farm and somehow got into town?

Mark took a careful step back, then another, wondering if he should simply turn and run. Or would that make the animal chase him down? He remembered footage of matadors being gored and trampled in the bullfight arena. His blood was pounding in his ears.

"Good morning!" called a woman walking two fat, panting Labradors up the path from the river. She paused to stand beside him, gazing at the large, brown beast. It had resumed cropping the grass under the trees, its head invisible once more.

"Hi!" he replied, without thinking, then asked, "What the hell is that thing doing here?"

"Oh, they bring a herd of cows in every summer to keep the grass down," said the woman. "Much better than using machinery, of course. They're quite harmless."

"But those horns," Mark protested, trying to hang onto some of his dignity. The two dogs sat looking up at him, tongues lolling, unfazed by the big beast a few feet away.

"Oh, it's definitely a cow," she assured him. "One of the older British breeds, which is why both sexes have horns. Evolution armed them for defense against predators! Something bred out of more modern varieties."

"Those horns look pretty dangerous," he said.

"Appearances can be deceptive, they really are amiable creatures," said the woman, resuming her walk.

I'm coming across like a dumb tourist, Mark thought. He set off along the path towards the Cam, wondering what other surprises the summer might have in store. Along the way he saw more cows, most of them taking advantage of the shade. None of them paid him the slightest attention.

***

"Another idiot," said Sharkey to himself. "Why can't some people learn to read the bloody signs?"

He stood on the edge of the landward-facing cliffs of Skara Farne, scanning the narrow strait between the island and the English coast. Sharkey's binoculars were old and in need of a good polish, but the old man's eyes were keen enough. Through the glasses he could make out the shape of a solitary cyclist riding onto the other end of the causeway that linked the island to the mainland or at least, linked it most of the time.

"There's a bloody great notice right there, man, and you've just gone sailing straight past it," muttered Sharkey.

The sign in question was large, a good four feet high with letters big enough to read without getting out of your car or, in this case, off your bike. It gave the times of high tides, which submerged the causeway for several hours a day. Sharkey didn't need written warnings. Like most native-born islanders he had an intuitive grasp of the rhythms of the moon-swollen sea. Whenever the tide was rising during the holiday season he made his way to the cliffs to check for people who, he felt, lacked the common sense that God gave the average goose.

"Damn fool!" he said, watching the cyclist for a few more moments, just to make sure the man didn't decide to go off the road and into the sand dunes for a picnic. People did sillier things. But no, this tourist was being a standard-issue clown, and simply trying to ride to Skara Farne along what looked like a clear road. Already the waves were washing over the dunes a mere ten yards to either side. Long before a man on a push-bike could make it to the island, the road would be awash.

Especially, thought Sharkey, *when what he's riding looks like it belongs in a ruddy museum.*

Sharkey lowered his binoculars and set off towards the lifeboat station a few hundred yards away. He could have called out the crew on general alert if he'd had one of those fancy new phones, but he didn't hold with that sort of thing. Besides, the official way to summon the crew was still to fire a maroon. And although he would never have admitted it to anyone, he got a great buzz out of the tremendous bang the signal rocket made when it exploded.

He was a man who enjoyed life's simple pleasures.

***

Mark crossed Midsummer Common and reached the Cam, then began walking along the riverbank path. He'd been aboard Dylan Morgan's boat before, but usually after dark and in a less-than-sober condition. His friend and colleagues tended to shift moorings now and again. Mark suspected but had never dared ask, that this was because Dylan sometimes needed to avoid the attentions of girlfriends who became too keen. Dozens of boats of various sizes were moored at Cambridge in summer. It was easy to tell the ones used as homes from the pleasure cruisers, as the latter didn't have bicycle racks or solar panels. But that still left rather a lot of houseboats to choose from.

Come on, where are you this week you old reprobate?

Then Mark had a stroke of luck. He spotted a patch of orange on one of the seats that lined the walkway. As he got closer, his initial guess was confirmed. It was Cassandra, Dylan's much-loved tabby cat, the only female creature he had ever fully committed to.

"Hey, there, Cass!" said Mark. The cat arched her back to be stroked.

Mark looked along the line of boats and, sure enough, Dylan's *Flower of Albion* was moored about ten yards away. Oddly though, when he set off toward it the cat didn't follow.

"You coming in for breakfast, Cass?" asked Mark.

Cassandra gave him a plaintive meow but stayed on the seat.

"Okay, suit yourself."

Who can fathom the ways of cats?

Dylan's home was a so-called 'narrow boat', a long, slender craft designed for England's extensive network of canals. It was low as well as narrow, and any unwary visitor over five feet tended to get bumps and bruises as a matter of routine. He clambered onto the deck and knocked on the tiny cabin door.

"Come in! I'm decent!" came a bellow from inside.

"I very much doubt that," replied Mark.

The exchange had become a ritual after Mark's first visit. Opening the cabin door, Mark remembered to duck and avoid the low ceiling, only to bark his shin against a chair lurking in the gloom. The smell of frying bacon emerged from the tiny galley up ahead.

"Take a seat, I won't be a moment. Can I get you anything?" called Dylan.

"Just coffee, I already ate," replied Mark, with an inward shudder at the thought of his friend's artery-hardening take on breakfast. He picked his way carefully to a bench as his eyes adjusted to the dim light.

After a minute, Dylan Morgan emerged from the galley with a well-laden tray. Mark took a mug of coffee and they exchanged a few more pleasantries before getting to the real purpose of this visit.

"I really appreciate this, Dylan," he said. "I appreciate that you could get in trouble with the college authorities over this."

Dylan shrugged.

"As my illustrious namesake would say, sod the lot of them."

Morgan, the senior lecturer in the English faculty, had been named after Dylan Thomas, a notoriously boozy and horny Welsh poet. Mark often wondered if he had deliberately taken on the Thomas persona or if it had just been a happy coincidence. Either way, Dylan Morgan was not one to play by the rules.

"The thing is," Dylan said, "the interview panel is going to decide whether you get another year as visiting professor, not just on the basis of your teaching, which is excellent, but also on your research. And I'm afraid the other candidates are looking a bit stronger on that front."

"I know," replied Mark, "it's just that, with adjusting to a new teaching role in a foreign country, I haven't had much time to do any research, let alone submit an academic paper."

"Publish or perish, old chap," said Dylan, shoving a fried

egg into a bun and adding a dollop of ketchup.

"You must produce something, otherwise your resume will be too thin and we won't be able to keep you on at St Caedmon's," pointed out Dylan. He bit into the fried egg sandwich, and yolk dribbled down his chin onto his ancient Ramones tee-shirt.

"Those things will kill you," said Mark.

"Well, at least I'll die fat and happy," replied Dylan, "making way for younger, leaner chaps like yourself. But you won't be able to fill my shoes at St Caedmon's unless you publish something!"

Mark spread his hands in a helpless gesture, not easy in the cramped cabin of Dylan's home, one of dozens of houseboats moored on the bank of the Cam.

"I appreciate you giving me the heads up, Dylan," he said, "but I'm fresh out of ideas. Of course, there's my chapter in the standard text on Gothic fiction ..."

Dylan shook his head.

"Not enough, just rehashing your greatest hits! You need to publish something new under your own name, a piece of original research. Preferably something that captures a bit of media interest."

Mark nodded. When Dylan had begun his career in teaching over two decades ago, the idea of a professor attracting good PR for the university would have seemed grotesque, demeaning. Now it was vital to put some kind of popular spin on everything you published to try and stay ahead of the game. But nothing Mark had been working on before he came to the UK was particularly newsworthy. 'Newsworthy' usually meant controversial or with a tie-in to a TV show or movie.

"Stumped, old chap?" asked Dylan, wiping egg off his tee-shirt with a paper napkin. "Well, what about looking into your illustrious predecessor?"

"Who? You mean the visiting professor from last year?" asked Mark, confused.

"No! I mean the chap who lived in your room in the college one hundred years back, give or take," said Dylan. "Here, let me find the damn book."

He began to rummage among the cardboard boxes of books that occupied much of the cabin space.

"How can you live like this?" asked Mark, trying to adjust his six-foot frame on the narrow bench seat.

"It's cheap and people leave you alone," replied Dylan. "I prefer being on the margins. Ah, here he is!"

He pulled out a book and tossed it across the tiny cabin. It was an old hardback volume without a dust jacket, and as Mark took it, he got the distinctive whiff of old paper familiar from innumerable second hand bookshops.

"A cheap wartime edition," explained Dylan. "No real value, poor quality paper and binding. But it contains all his best-known stories."

Mark opened the book, flipped to the title page, and read.

The Dark Isle & Other Ghost Stories by Montague Summerskill, D.Litt, FRSA

"So this guy lived in my room at St Caedmon's?" he asked, reading the list of story titles. "How come I've never heard of him?"

"Simple," said Dylan, "he died before he could finish his second collection of tales, so he was a bit of a one-hit wonder. That's his only book, and it was published at the outbreak of the First World War, so it was rather overshadowed by world events despite excellent reviews. It's a lost classic, in my humble opinion. I don't think it's currently in print anywhere. Having said that, a few of the tales in it have been anthologized. And I think a couple were dramatized by the BBC ages ago, back in the black and white era when they did ghost stories every Christmas."

Mark turned to the middle of the book and read a few sentences of Summerskill's prose in a story entitled 'The Burial Mound'.

I found myself possessed of the conviction that I had stumbled upon something best left undisturbed. For several minutes, I had had the definite sensation that I was being closely observed, and yet whenever I turned around to scan the moors around me I could not see a soul. This should have reassured me, but instead I found myself wondering if some furtive watcher or watchers might be using the lie of the land to conceal themselves while keeping me under scrutiny.

"This seems fairly standard stuff for the period," said Mark, dubiously. "A bit stodgy; is there anything unusual about the book I might get a paper out of?"

"The author is arguably as interesting as the book. Look him up," said Dylan, with a smug expression. "Go on, Google him on your fancy gadget."

Mark took out his phone and quickly found a short biography of Montague Summerskill. He had been a Fellow of the Royal Society of Antiquaries and an 'amateur author of supernatural fiction, drawing upon his extensive knowledge of history and folklore to give his tales the ring of authenticity'.

"So what?" asked Mark, looking up from the screen.

"Keep going, right to the end," said Dylan.

Mark scrolled down the page and almost went past a paragraph entitled 'Death: Mysterious Circumstances'. He read it then re-read it, before looking back at his friend.

"A writer of supernatural fiction died of drowning on dry land after being attacked by some sort of monster? In front of witnesses? Come on!"

Dylan shrugged.

"I admit it seems absurd, but isn't it just the sort of angle you need to make a short paper on Summerskill's fiction into, oh, what do they call it now? Click-bait? Awful term, sounds too much like jail-bait for my liking."

"Well," said Mark, "I suppose if he did die in weird circumstances that would be a good hook. I could hang a decent paper on that. The guy's output was small. And my just happening to live in his apartment is a good detail too, sort of thing reporters like."

"Now you're getting it!" said Dylan. "Go off and throw something together, just a one-page summary, have it ready for the interview."

They chatted for a few minutes longer, and Mark began to warm up to the thought of a paper on Summerskill. Then an idea struck him.

"It says here a lot of his stories were based on visits to different parts of England on cycling holidays, where he learned about local folklore and legends. Maybe I could re-enact some of his journeys, blog about it? That would be a good angle, especially if I could get some of my students onboard."

"Now you're talking!" said Dylan. "Get it going viral, isn't that the term? An American in Limey-land, looking for the real-life spooks that might have bumped off a ghost story author. Blog yourself senseless, lad, they'll lap it up!"

They chatted a while longer, then Mark had to leave for his last tutorial of the semester. He thanked Dylan again, put the Summerskill book in his laptop bag, and climbed ashore from the *Flower of Albion* feeling buoyed up by the informal get-together. It was good to have a 'friend at court' as the Brits put it. Someone you knew was batting for you.

He decided to take the same route back to St Caedmon's College and set off along the riverside walk. Cassandra was still on the bench and watched him approach, her tail a-twitch.

"Hey, Cass, your lord and master is well and truly awake!" he said. "He's probably got a nice can of tuna lined up for you."

Mark reached out to pet the tabby, but instead of arching her back she flinched, hissed and spat, then leaped down from the bench and ran to Dylan's boat.

Cats are weird at the best of times, he thought, his feelings slightly hurt. He watched Cassandra leap aboard through an open porthole, then set off back across Midsummer Common. He was ready for the cows this time, but it seemed they weren't ready for him. The animals looked up as he approached and, with bellows of what seemed like alarm, quickly moved aside, well away from the path Mark was taking.

Cows and cats find me repulsive, he thought. *Maybe I should change my aftershave.*

Chapter 2: Ghosts and Scholars

After a slow start to the afternoon, the bar of the Grey Horse was suddenly crowded, thanks to the arrival of the volunteer lifeboat crew.

"Another tourist stuck in a sweatbox, was it?" asked Rose Hyde, pulling pints of the local beer.

The 'sweatboxes' were small huts mounted on ten-foot stilts near the middle of the causeway, allowing people trapped by the tide to climb up a ladder and wait for rescue. As the nickname suggested, the huts hadn't been designed for comfort. They sometimes ended up smelling of worse things than sweat.

"Not exactly," said Jim Falk, the captain of the lifeboat. He gave a slight jerk of the head to indicate the end of the bar where Sharkey was nursing his pint alone.

"Another false alarm?" asked Rose, lowering her voice.

"Too bloody right!" said another crew member, without moderating his tone. "We spent two friggin' hours farting around out there. Not a trace of anybody. 'Bloke on an old-fashioned bicycle' my arse!"

Sharkey didn't look round, but silently picked up his pint and went outside.

"You should cut him some slack, lads," said Rose. "He's been through a lot."

"I know," replied Jim, but there were derisive noises from other life boatmen.

"If you're seeing things, you shouldn't be on the crew, simple as that," said one, to murmurs of agreement.

"Well, Barry," shot back Rose, "judging by your state most Saturday nights, we're lucky you don't call the boat out to look for pink elephants."

That got a good laugh and lightened the mood somewhat. Leaving the crew to their banter, Rose went outside to collect glasses and found Sharkey standing by the wall of the small beer garden, looking out at the causeway.

"Al right, Sharkey?" she asked.

He didn't reply.

Rose put the glasses down on a table and went up to him, touched him on the shoulder.

"I know you saw it, Sharkey."

"Don't you go and humor me, girl," he muttered, lips barely moving under his straggling gray beard.

"Brown clothes, maybe tweed. Cycle clips, thick socks. Cloth cap, with a peak. Old-fashioned bike, clunky-looking," said Rose.

Sharkey looked down at her, eyes wide.

Rose turned away, picked up the glasses and said over her shoulder.

"You're not the only one with the sight, Sharkey. I've seen that one a few times lately. The closer to the edge we get, one way or another, the more likely we are to see them. They're nothing to be scared of, just you remember that."

Sharkey watched her as she went inside, then turned and took a swig of his beer and set the glass back down on the wall.

"It's not the ghosts I'm scared of, girl," he said to himself, as he watched the shifting patterns of the restless sea.

***

Mark's last tutorial of the year was a small affair, attended by just three of his most enthusiastic students. His American Gothic Fiction course had been well-attended, a fact Dylan had predictably attributed to Mark's 'magnetic personality and devastating good looks'. The truth, Mark told himself, was simply that the subject was intrinsically fascinating and that he managed to convey his enthusiasm for it.

"Okay, guys, this is kind of a formality," said Mark, sitting down at the head of the table in the small tutorial room. "Your assignments were all pretty darn good, and I'm sure you've got nothing to worry about when you start your final year."

This endorsement didn't get much of a reaction. Mark had become used to British reserve in the last nine months or so. Most natives carried around thick layers of emotional armor. Heavy irony and thinly-veiled sarcasm were more likely than enthusiasm from any but the most outgoing Brit.

Everything has to be played down. Still, one of them

might have cracked a smile, he thought.

Mark looked around the table. The only male student, Sebastian, was looking down at his folded hands. The two young women, Juliet and Katrina, seemed out of it entirely. Juliet, normally as loud as her purple-dyed hair, was gazing at a point somewhere above, behind Mark's head. Katrina, petite and frail-seeming, was nibbling her fingernails and staring blankly at her tutor, giving no sign of having heard his praise. It was hard not to think of Katrina as a schoolgirl who had somehow strayed into university and was doing her best to fit in.

"Right," said Mark, taking a breath, "any questions on Ambrose Bierce?"

There was a pause then Juliet asked, "Do you think he believed in all that stuff?"

"Believed in all what stuff?" asked Mark, puzzled.

"In the supernatural; in ghosts ... that kind of thing."

Juliet's voice was oddly flat, nothing like her normal hearty tones. She tended to be combative in a positive way, providing the energy for discussions.

Maybe she's ill? Hell, maybe some kind of summer virus is going round the campus and it will ruin my vacation!

Before Mark could frame an answer, Sebastian snorted and said, "Of course not, the man was a professional newspaper hack! Ambrose Bierce spent most of his life scandal-mongering and mud-slinging. He even disappeared in Mexico in search of a political story. He wrote what would sell, he didn't let beliefs get in the way. If he had any beliefs, of course."

The student leaned back as if he had just won a brilliant debate. Mark had struggled to like Sebastian, but had given up about halfway through the course and decided to simply tolerate the boy's arrogance and leave it to life to rub some edges off him. But he couldn't let an ignorant remark pass.

"As you may recall from my lecture, Sebastian," he said, "Bierce didn't make much money from his ghost stories and other macabre fiction. He kept returning to the subject of the supernatural at a time when it wasn't commercially viable, during the so-called Gilded Age when brassy materialism was the norm. And a perfectly poised story such as 'The Eyes of the Panther' is hardly hackwork."

Mark paused. Normally this kind of authoritative statement would be the cue for a discussion among the well-read youngsters. Not today. Sebastian gave a smirk but didn't rise to the bait, Katrina carried on biting her nails, while Juliet shook her head in agreement but said nothing, choosing instead to gaze out of the window.

"Oh-kay," said Mark, "Since you guys are all talked out, let's just check your final grades. If you have any queries on your final assignments I'll be happy to answer them. Remember, there's an appeals process, but you've got to get your request in before the deadline, which is the end of next month. Not that any of you guys need to, of course, it's just a formality I have to tell you about. Then we're done, and you can go off and enjoy your summer."

He opened his bag and put his laptop onto the desk. As he put the bag to one side the Summerskill hardback fell out onto the desk with a surprisingly loud thud.

"Woops! That's my holiday reading, better not lose it," he said, shoving the old book back into the bag.

Mark spent a few seconds booting up his laptop, but when he looked up again he saw that Juliet was staring at his bag, eyes wide. Even more oddly, Katrina had stopped biting her nails and was looking back and forth between Juliet and the bag. Only Sebastian was acting normally, for him at least. He was still smirking, but there was a hint of puzzlement.

"Everything okay, guys?" Mark asked. Juliet mumbled something that might have been 'No worries' and resumed her study of the college courtyard. Katrina looked Mark straight in the eye and seemed about to speak, then looked at Sebastian and clearly thought better of it.

"Okay, final grades," said Mark. This seemed to return the girls to normal, and the tutorial ended without further incidents. Mark wished his students goodbye, and stood up. The girls shot out of the room with hasty farewells, leaving Sebastian packing up at a more leisurely pace.

"They've been totally weird these last few weeks," remarked the young man.

"In what way?" asked Mark.

"Going off into corners, having serious conversations. If I didn't know better, I'd say they were having a bumpy patch in a passionate relationship."

"But you know better?" returned Mark.

"Oh yes, Juliet is definitely straight, in that punchy feminist way of hers," replied Sebastian. "Kat, I wouldn't know about her, she's as timid as a church mouse."

"Maybe they're ill, is something going round?"

Sebastian's reply was in an even more sarcastic tone than usual.

"Whatever it is I don't think a dose of antibiotics is what's required. Anyway, have a good holiday! I know I will."

"You too," said Mark, trying to sound sincere.

After Sebastian left, Mark went to the window and looked out onto the grassy court, surrounded on all sides by 14th century college buildings. It was a comforting view, and he knew it symbolized the kind of continuity he had always sought in his life, but never found until now.

God, I'm so simple, sometimes. I feel I belong here because I've never felt like I belonged anywhere else.

This took him back to the Sue problem, and how he would break the news that he wanted to stay in Cambridge for another year. He was so preoccupied that he didn't notice Juliet until he almost walked into her. She was standing by the door into the court.

"Sorry, Mark," she said quickly, "I just wanted to say, erm, have a good break! And it's been good having you as our tutor. And lecturer, of course."

"Thanks!" he said, "Have you got any plans for the vacation?"

She shook her head impatiently.

"No, nothing special, but look," she began, then stopped, looked down at his laptop bag.

"You should give that book straight back to the old bastard!"

Then she turned and ran off towards the main-gate.

"What do you mean?" he called after Juliet. She showed no sign of having heard him, and seconds later had vanished into the busy streets of Cambridge.

"Right," he said to himself, baffled. "The summer vacation begins and student crazy time is well and truly upon us."

He reached into the bag, took out the Summerskill and flipped through it as if it might contain a clue to his student's behavior. Of course there was nothing unusual about it. Except now, that he looked more closely, he saw some faint scribbles on one of the blank pages at the very end of the book. It was a spidery scrawl, but he could just make out the words.

Wrong edition! Try Gadabout '87.

The name 'Gadabout' meant nothing to him. He recalled it was an old-fashioned term for wanderer or a seeker. But here it was capitalized. Maybe, given the context, it was an obscure publisher.

Mark shrugged. He could always look it up later. And it didn't explain Juliet's apparent antipathy to the long-dead Montague Summerskill.

Stowing away the book he crossed the court, heading for the stairway that led up to his rooms. As he did so, he saw one of the inevitable tourist parties being ushered out of the building, blocking the entrance. With a sigh he resigned himself to wait while the guide, whom he didn't recognize, gave his spiel about St Caedmon's history. Mark had heard it, read it, even delivered some of it himself to tourists who tended to wander off the official route and asked random questions to anyone they met.

The party in this case consisted of a dozen Spanish tourists, all well-equipped with maps, leaflets, and of course cameras. One boy of about twelve was filming everything in sight, and inevitably Mark came into his viewfinder. Mark smiled, gave a polite wave, and the boy waved back. Then the child stopped filming and looked, puzzled, at his camera. He turned and tugged at a man's sleeve, evidently asking for help from his father. The boy was shushed for his troubles.

The guide finished describing a particularly grisly execution for heresy that had taken place in the 16th century and led his party away.

Mark could go in now, but he suddenly felt an odd reluctance to go up the narrow, poorly-lit stairway. He found himself standing, staring at a weathered gargoyle over the door.

I don't want to be alone in the dark.

The thought came out of nowhere, and give him a genuine shiver up the spine. He shook off the eerie sensation and went inside.

I really do need a break from teaching Gothic fiction, he thought. *A few weeks traveling round the countryside will do me good. And reading some stodgy old English ghost stories, putting together a paper on them. Yeah, why not? Just enough work amid the leisure to keep me on my toes.*

***

"Manuel, if you do not take that camera off the table I will confiscate it!" said his father, using his extra calm don't-push-me voice that he reserved for public places, like this restaurant.

"Oh, leave the poor boy alone," said his mother, pausing in her struggle with a cheeseburger, "isn't it bad enough that you should drag a child around these boring old buildings? Let him play with his toy!"

Manuel wanted to protest that it wasn't a toy and he wasn't playing. But he knew that if he claimed that he was studying a fascinating paranormal phenomenon he would never see his camera again until they got back to Barcelona, if he was lucky. He lowered the shiny gadget below the level of the table and shoved french fries into his mouth with one hand while working the controls with the other.

The camcorder's LCD screen was frustratingly small and most of the clip in question was taken up with the friendly Englishman who had waited so patiently for the dull man to finish talking. He restarted the video and watched again, knowing now to focus his attention on the top right of the glowing rectangle. There it was! A vaguely man-shaped blur that seemed to ripple and twist in the air as it shot into focus for an instant, hovered behind the man, then sped off to the left toward the gates of the college.

The next time he ran the clip, Manuel managed to freeze

the frame and zoom in. The bigger he made the image, the more the thing looked like a person.

Only not the kind of person you would like to meet, he thought. *Can it be a ghost?*

Manuel had seen so many bad ghost pictures and videos on the internet that he knew nobody would believe this one was real. But it had really been there. It was so frustrating. Perhaps an expert could be found online who would testify to its authenticity?

At maximum zoom, the image was very grainy, individual pixels clearly visible. The face of the 'ghost' was merely a vague block of gray and brown squares, like some of the modern art Father insisted on taking them to see.

Then the face began to move. The squares vanished to be replaced by a well-defined face, a grinning visage that would haunt Manuel's nightmares for years to come. He dropped the camcorder.

"Well," said his father, glancing down, "that's one hundred and twenty Euros wasted. I hope you're satisfied."

"Never mind," said Manuel's mother soothingly, leaning down to pick up the pieces. "Perhaps we can find a clever man who will fix it."

Manuel, pale-faced and trembling, shook his head.

"No!" he shouted. "Leave the monster in there! It has seen me!"

It took the grown-ups a good ten minutes to calm him down.

***

"I should never have burned it!" said Katrina, staring at her untouched coffee. Juliet reached out and took her friend's hand in hers.

"Come on, Kat, you've got to be strong! We can do this together!"

The smaller girl shook her head. She was almost in tears. Juliet felt anger surge up on her friend's behalf, but it was mixed with frustration at Katrina's passivity. They were sitting in Juliet's room in their shared student house on the outskirts of Cambridge. For the hundredth time, Juliet was trying and failing to persuade her friend to do something; not merely be a helpless victim.

"We can't let him get away with this kind of shit! If you go to the authorities, I'll support you, and then we can tell him to stuff his mind games!"

Katrina's only response was to shake her head again, and then look past Juliet out of the window. Juliet didn't turn round.

"You've been frightened into seeing things!" she insisted, squeezing Katrina's hand even more tightly. "You've let him get into your head, the way you let him—"

Katrina jumped up and rushed out of the pub, Juliet following despite her friend's protests.

"I just want to be alone, it's not safe for you!"

"Don't be daft," replied Juliet, "it's all down to suggestion, like voodoo or something. Nothing like that can really hurt you unless you let it."

Katrina stood hesitating on the sidewalk then her phone gave a chirrup.

"It's another text," she said, picking up the phone from the tabletop.

"Just more intimidation," insisted Juliet. "We can take this to a tribunal and they'll sack him, really. You just need to ... What is it? Kat?"

But Katrina was staring at the small screen. She turned the phone around so Juliet could see the text message.

99 Days Were Allowed.

"More mind games!" said Juliet. "Look, we need to go back to college right now and get this sorted before all the bigwigs go on leave."

Katrina was staring past Juliet at the door of the apartment.

"It's here!" she whispered. "I thought it had gone, left me alone, but that was just a trick! It's back now, and it's going to—"

There was a loud knocking at the door, and both girls

jumped.

"Hey," came a man's voice, "you two brainiacs coming to the pub?"

"No, thanks," shouted Juliet, relief in her voice.

"Suit yourselves. See you later!"

They heard footsteps retreating down the hallway.

"See?" said Juliet. "We'll be jumping at shadows, next."

"Maybe you're right," said Katrina, picking up her coffee with her free hand. She took a sip. "Yeuch, that's cold."

"Since the kitchen is free, we can make some more, maybe make some lunch," suggested Juliet.

"I think I'll have some juice instead," replied Katrina. "It seems to be getting really hot in here."

***

Lucy finished her shift at the Gray Horse at one and set off home, a walk of about two miles. She was passing the site of the old abbey when she spotted a figure stooping amid the heaps of ancient masonry. On an impulse, she climbed over the low fence and made her way over to where Victor Carew was performing some obscure task on the site of what had been, centuries earlier, the altar of the Abbot's private chapel.

"Treasure hunting?" she asked as she came up behind the old man.

He stood up and she saw that he held a sheet of paper and a piece of charcoal. He had evidently been taking rubbings of the base of the long-vanished altar. The overgrown rectangle of granite was easily overlooked but a lot of strange stories seemed to cling to it.

"Trying to solve a minor mystery," he replied. "And I might point out that the Red Abbey is closed to visitors."

"You going to report me for trespassing?" she asked. "Or just administer corporal punishment here and now?"

Carew rolled his eyes.

"You young women today, shameless!" he said. "Here, take a look."

He handed her the paper and she examined it, frowning. The rubbing was of the four odd carvings on the base of the altar. They had been almost erased by exposure to the elements over nearly five centuries, but were still the most intriguing feature of the ruined abbey.

"I thought we'd agreed they represent the four seasons?" asked Lucy.

"You agreed. I went along with you for the sake of a quiet life," replied Carew.

Since he had taken over the job of curator for the charitable trust that owned the Red Abbey, Carew and Lucy had become firm friends. They had a mutual interest in the less-traveled byways of history and folklore, plus a similarly irreverent sense of humor. And, what was more, they were outsiders, not island-born. That counted for a lot on Skara Farne.

Lucy turned the paper around, treating it like a magic eye picture. The charcoal rubbings showed four faint outlines in roughly square frames. There were pictures there, if you sort of squinted and used a lot of imagination. One seemed to show a face with swollen cheeks blowing out a gust of wind. In another, an almost featureless shape was emerging from what looked like waves. A third had a vertical pattern suggestive of flames, while the fourth was almost blank.

"Now I agree that the first might show the autumn winds," said Carew, "And perhaps the flames might represent summer heat. But what about the water?"

"Winter storms? We are on an island, after all," she pointed out. "But I agree, we are reaching a little. So what might they be if they're not the four seasons?" she asked.

"Something even more fundamental," replied Carew. "The very stuff of reality according to the ancient philosophers. Think back to the Greeks, how significant the number four was to them. Humor me!"

Lucy stared at the paper again, and suddenly grasped what he meant.

Humor me, she thought. *Oh, very clever!*

***

"You're right, it is getting hotter," said Juliet, washing out two glasses while Katrina got some orange juice from the fridge. "I wouldn't mind but the place is like the North Pole in winter. We should get onto that landlord, make him fix up some kind of air conditioning. This can't be legal." Juliet reached out to open the small window, then pulled her hand back with a cry of surprise. There was a red welt across her fingers and thumb.

"What is it?" asked Katrina, standing at the fridge door.

"That window catch, it's red hot!"

They stared at the metal catch as if it could explain itself.

"I suppose it is in direct sunlight," said Juliet, dubiously. "God, it's so warm in here. I'll open the back door, let some heat out."

But before she could move towards the door, Katrina screamed, dropped the orange juice carton, and backed into the nearest corner. At first, Juliet had no idea what her friend was staring at, wide-eyed with terror. Then she saw what looked like a swirl of glowing dust motes in the air.

"It's nothing, Kat, don't be so jumpy," she said, but without much conviction.

This is not natural, Juliet thought. *Oh Christ, what if it's all true, all that stuff about the curse?*

The temperature in the room was sweltering now, and most of the heat seemed to radiate from the strange vortex, which was growing brighter. Juliet retreated towards the door that led into the main part of the house and grabbed the handle. This time she screamed in agony as her flesh was seared with heat. She tried to pull her hand away and felt skin tearing.

"Oh, God!" Juliet doubled up in pain, staring in baffled terror while the glowing whirlwind of fiery particles grew, coalesced, and took shape. It became a roughly human form limned in yellow-white fire. It was so bright that it rivaled the midday sunlight. The kitchen was as hot as a furnace, and Juliet felt her hair and eyebrows start to singe, almost distracting her from the pain from her burnt hand.

Katrina was crouching in the corner, arms crossed over her face, trying to make herself even smaller. She made a keening sound, wordless, like a frightened child. The fire-being moved towards her, its blazing arms outstretched. Katrina's hair and blouse started to smoke.

"Get away from her!" Juliet shouted, but she was paralyzed by pain and terror.

The incandescent entity enveloped Katrina, and Juliet saw her friend's clothes and hair burst into flames as the girl's flesh darkened and shriveled. The cramped kitchen filled with the smell of charred meat. Juliet lost all control, wrapped a kitchen towel around her good hand, and tried again to open the door. The cloth burst into flames and the heat from the metal took off more strips of flesh. Juliet turned round just in time to look into the dazzling eyes of the fire-being before it wrapped her in its embrace.

Chapter 3: Telling Stories

Mike spent an hour and a half putting together a rough proposal for a paper on Montague Summerskill, but soon realized that he could only bluff so much.

Guess I'll have to actually read the old fart's stories at some point, he thought. *Ah well, at least it's a short book, nice big print. No time like the present.*

He got a sandwich from the fridge, made some coffee, and then flung himself down onto his narrow, hard mattress to start reading *The Dark Isle & Other Ghost Stories.* Rather than start with the title story, which ran to nineteen pages, he plumped for the shortest tale, 'Lost on the Moors'. In style, it was as old-fashioned as he expected, but still fun in a slightly camp way. He settled down to give it his full attention.

The story was about a middle-aged academic, obviously a surrogate for the author, bicycling across the Yorkshire Moors on a midsummer night. Predictably enough, he gets lost and ends up seeking shelter at a remote farmhouse where a very old woman offers him a bed for the night. She tells him to stay in his room, especially between the hours of midnight and two, because 'in the witching hour, the dead might work their will upon the living'.

"Yeah, the twist will be that she's a ghost," said Mark to himself. He hadn't hoped for much, but so far this was really clichéd stuff, the kind of thing kids churn out all the time for Creepypasta.

But Summerskill had a surprise in store. Mark read on to the point where the traveler hears his watch chime midnight, and then there's a knock at his door. When he answers, the woman's voice asks him if he has everything he needs. There's something odd about her voice, though, and this prompts the man to get up and open the door. By the light of a candle, Summerskill's narrator sees standing there, not the old crone who let him into the house but a beautiful young woman. Yet she is wearing the same shabby dress and shawl as the old woman and the resemblance between the two is so striking that he 'could not doubt for a moment that they were, in some unimaginable sense, one and the same.'

"Whoa!" said Mark, impressed despite his earlier cynicism.

The lovely young woman tells the traveler that she is afraid to spend the night alone in the haunted cottage. Not surprisingly, even an English gentleman hesitates to turn her away, but is unable to bring himself to step back from the threshold and let her in. She reaches out and takes his hand, presses it to her warm cheek.

Wow, this is strong stuff for its day, Mark thought. *Maybe Monty wasn't such a boring old fart after all? I'll have to check if there's more information about his private life. Just because he was a bachelor didn't mean he lived like a monk.*

The ending comes when the traveler leans forward to kiss the woman, emitting 'a gasp of astonishment' that blows out the candle. Then he feels 'the warm, velvety flesh of her cheek turn to wrinkled parchment, her soft little hand become a leathery claw.' Reeling back from the encounter the traveler strikes his head on the bedstead. As he loses consciousness, his last sensation is of 'sour breath on his face and wizened hands working desperately at the buttons of his nightshirt.' He awakens in the morning light, fully clothed, lying alongside his bike in the ruins of a cottage 'long overgrown with nettles and heather.'

'It had surely not been inhabited for many decades,' concludes the author.

"Boom! No trite explanation, so the mystery lingers in the mind. How very modern," said Mark approvingly, getting up to pour himself another mug of coffee. If Summerskill's other stories were as accomplished, then a paper might actually be a pleasure to write. *Hell, I might even work in a feminist angle on that one,* he thought.

Mark lay back down, book open on his chest, pondering how to revise his proposal. He must have dozed off, because suddenly the room was dark, all trace of midday sunshine gone.

Crap, he thought. *Too many late nights marking papers catching up with me.*

35

Then he realized he wasn't alone.

The only armchair in the room was in the corner, facing the bed, in the deep shadow beside the window. In the uncertain gray light Mark could only be sure that there was someone sitting in the armchair, someone tall and rangy with broad shoulders.

"Hi, Markie," said his visitor. The voice was familiar.

"Billy?" said Mark, sitting up. "Billy Straker? That you?"

"Large as life and twice as ugly," said Billy, with chuckle.

"My God, it's so good to see you!" said Mark, swinging his legs off the bed. "But what the Hell are you doing in England?"

"You think they wouldn't let me in?" asked Billy. "Maybe. I'm a real dangerous guy!"

Again that chuckle, so familiar, unheard for so many years.

Mark hesitated. A memory was darting around, just out of reach, defying his mind's efforts to snare it. Something about Billy; why they had not seen one another for so long.

"Thing is," Billy went on, "they can't put me on a no-fly list. For obvious reasons."

Mark clicked on the lamp by his bedside, and saw his old friend clearly for the first time.

Billy was still dressed in the way he had favored in high school. Football shirt, cut-off denims, sneakers. But that wasn't what struck Mark as unusual. No, the unusual thing was the reddish-black stain almost obliterating the number 18 in the middle of his shirt, coupled with the small round hole just above Billy's left eye.

"Yep, they got me, gangster style," said Billy. "Three in the body, one in the head. Sending a message, I guess. A bit late for me to learn anything from it, though."

This time he didn't chuckle.

***

Lucy Hyde carried her shopping up the spiral staircase of the old lighthouse, occasionally putting her free hand on the cool curving wall. She didn't really need to lean on the old building for support, but it comforted her to feel the sheer strength of the tower; its permanence.

All illusory, of course, she thought. *Nothing really lasts. Some things simply perish sooner than others.*

She reached her bedroom which lay just beneath the old lamp gallery, where the light had shined out to warn ships off the Farne Islands decades earlier. The room was Spartan, equipped with two bunk beds, a table, and two chairs. Lighthouses were superfluous to requirements in this world of computers and satellite navigation, of course. But for that precise reason, Lucy felt a strong sense of kinship with her unusual home.

We're both obsolete, she thought, gazing out over cliffs at the iron-gray North Sea. *Both part of a world that's supposedly dead and gone, abolished by progress. But guess what? We're both still here.*

Lucy turned away from the small window and sat down at the table, opened a pinewood box, removed a deck of large, ornately-decorated cards. She pondered for a moment, then shuffled the cards, dealt a spread of seven in a cross pattern with the cards face down. Then she began to turn the cards over, one by one.

"Deceit," she said. "Treachery. A journey? The Fool."

A black cat that had been sleeping on the upper bunk got up, stretched, and leaped easily onto the table. It placed a paw on the one Tarot card that was still face down. Lucy turned it over. It showed a tower being struck by lightning, screaming people plunging through the air as the structure collapsed.

"Oh, Basil," she said, "whose side are you on, anyway?"

The cat began to wash its face.

***

Mark's legs failed him and sat down heavily on the bed.

"You can't be here, Billy," he protested, wondering if he was going crazy. "You've been dead for fifteen years."

"I know," said Billy, standing up. "It's a pisser, believe me."

"But why are you here now?" Mark asked.

His murdered friend shrugged.

"Disturbance in the Force, Markie! It's out there, churning up us ghosts. Like a jet-plane, I guess, or a speedboat, it leaves a hell of a wake."

"What's out there?" asked Mark.

Billy shrugged again.

"Beats the crap outta me. All I know is, it's got you in its sights. Take care, Markie."

There was a knock at the door.

Mark was lying on the bed in a room filled with sunlight. Summerskill's book had fallen onto the floor. The chair by the window was empty, of course.

For a couple of seconds Mark froze, then laughed.

God, that was a hell of a daydream, he thought. *Maybe I have been overworking.*

The knocking resumed, louder now.

"Who is it?" he called.

"It's me, Doctor! I do for you now!"

Mark admitted Elena the garrulous Polish cleaner. He'd forgotten she was due this afternoon.

"Sorry, I'll get out of your way," he said, picking *The Dark Isle* off the carpet.

"No, no, you stay, I work round you!" insisted Elena, lugging her cleaning gear into the already cramped kitchenette. "You keep me company, we have nice chat like sensible British people, yes?"

In the event, the chat consisted of Elena delivering a running commentary on both her personal troubles and those of the wider world in an accent so thick that Mark would have struggled to respond even if she had given him an opening. He ended up half-listening to her while thumbing through the Summerskill book, hoping to hit on more passages with overtly sexual overtones. Then something Elena said made him interrupt her and ask,

"Sorry, what did you say? A fire?"

"Those poor girls! You teach them maybe? These greedy landlords, I know them, they are very bad men, never fix up those houses properly."

"What girls?" Mark asked, but he had a terrible feeling that he already knew.

"The tall one with blue hair and her friend, the pretty little one who is quiet like mouse! I see them in cafe where I work sometime. They were nice polite girls, not wild like some. Always polite, always leave tip."

"Do you mean Juliet and Katrina? What's happened to them?" he asked. But then his phone rang, and he soon had more details than even Elena could provide.

***

Detective Sergeant Jo Garland tried to settle into the chair opposite her superior. Rumor at Cambridgeshire Police HQ had it that Superintendent Masson had tested out a dozen chairs and picked the most uncomfortable from the official catalog to make his subordinates squirm, even when they had nothing to squirm about.

In this case, she reflected, *some squirming may be inevitable.*

"The Fire Investigators are sure it didn't start in the wiring or any of the kitchen appliances, sir," she stated, flatly.

"But it definitely did start in the kitchen?"

Masson frowned at the scene-of-crime pictures, set them down next to his lunchtime coffee and bacon sandwich.

Will I ever get to be so casual about violent deaths? Jane wondered. *Just another day at the office, but two people happened to have burnt to death?*

"So, there's a possibility that it was arson?" asked Masson, his frown deepening.

"Not really, sir, as there was no trace of accelerant. The only unusual feature–" Jo began.

"Was that the two very intelligent girls didn't simply leave the kitchen when the fire started, using either of the two entrances, neither of which were locked or obstructed in any way," cut in Masson. "I have done this before, Sergeant. There are always a few weird ones in anyone's career. The trick is not to overthink them. We're not exactly short of crimes we could definitely solve, if we just had the time and resources."

He stood up, went to the window, and looked out at the city, now bustling with midday shoppers, workers on lunch breaks, and the inevitable throng of tourists.

"One thing you never get used to is breaking the news to the parents," he said. "Foul play requires suspects, Jo. Do you have any?"

She took a deep breath, and said, "Well, sir, the other student in the house was definitely not at home, he'd invited them out for a drink and was in the pub with his mates when the neighbor called 999."

"I'm not talking about routine stuff, Jo," said Masson, turning to lean against the window sill. "I mean is your instinct telling you there's something wrong here?"

"Yes, sir," she replied, without thinking. "There's something odd about this one. I've checked both victims' internet activity and there are some anomalies. Emails from addresses that don't seem to exist anymore, that kind of thing."

Masson sighed.

"God, I hate the internet! Life was so much simpler when criminals just wrote threatening letters or kept nice detailed journals of their vile antics. Now we have to chase the evil buggers through cyberspace. Anything else?"

Jo hesitated, then said, "The last person to talk to them, as far as we know, was their lecturer."

"Ah, yes, this Stine person," said Masson, picking up a document. "Here on a work visa, I see. What about him?"

"I just got an odd sort of vibe off him, sir," replied Jo. "Nothing definite. He was shocked, of course, and that seemed genuine enough. But I got the impression that he was holding something back."

"That's it?" asked Masson, sitting down again. "He's a foreign national, so if we want to check his background, I have to go through Interpol. Which means higher clearance, and budgetary issues. All on your gut instinct."

"I know, sir," said Jo. "I just thought–"

"Feel free to think, as long as it costs us nothing," cut in Masson. He gave a thin smile, then, and said in a voice that was almost warm. "It's a good report, you've done all right. First major case, if you go on like this you've got a decent career ahead of you. But remember it's evidence that makes a case, not gut instinct. Dismissed."

After the young detective left, Masson looked at the photos of the victims again. His own daughter was at university, though not in Cambridge. He took out an old-fashioned address book, looked up a number, and dialed it.

"Hello?" he said, when he got through. "Could you tell Special Agent Fox that Barry Masson called, from England? Yes, England. Well, please get him to contact me as soon as possible, I'll give you the number. What's it about? Well, tell him I'm finally calling in the favor he owes me."

***

"Let's get this straight," said Sue. "You're planning to stay in England? Like, indefinitely? To live?"

Mark wished he could reach through the screen and hug Sue, hold her close, and tell her he wanted to live in England with her. *That would be my perfect life,* he thought. *The right place with the right person, and Sue's god-awful family at least fifteen hours away by air.*

Instead, he put on a conciliatory tone and said, "Honey, I can't pass up a great career opportunity. I got to put 'Visiting Professor' on my resume already, but two years at Cambridge, that beats anything on offer Stateside!"

"I thought you were coming home," she said, with a trace of a sniffle. "I thought we'd spend the summer vacation together."

"We still can," he insisted, deciding to play his ace. "You can come and visit me here, make it a really great holiday."

"I don't know," she said, but he thought there was a trace of enthusiasm. She had often talked about visiting Europe. As a professional photographer specializing in historic buildings and landscapes, it would be like a trip to the candy store for her.

"Sue, why not come over and we can stay in London, maybe take a trip to Paris, or spend a couple of days in Rome? Anything you like."

"I can't get away until late summer," she said. She sounded uncertain to Mark but no longer obviously upset.

He explained that late summer was fine, as he had a project that would occupy him for the next few weeks.

"You're such a workaholic!" she said, smiling now. "But you're not the only one with a career."

"I know," he said, "and maybe I won't be able to cut it here. But I want to at least give it a try."

The screen flickered, then Sue's image froze. Mark cursed the Wi-Fi the college provided. It was free but erratic. He resisted the temptation to start mouse-clicking or pounding random keys and waited for the thing to sort itself out.

"Come on, come on," he said under his breath, trying to hold down his techno-rage.

The screen unfroze, and Sue's expression changed instantly from mild worry to puzzlement.

"What was that, Mark?" she asked.

"Sorry," he replied, "the connection is real glitchy here."

"No, not that," she said. "Who was that old guy standing behind you? One of your British pals? He looked like he was going to a costume ball in that old suit."

"Aw, it was probably just somebody jerking us around, you know. Hackers, student pranksters," he said, trying to sound sure of himself. "Look, think about what I said. It's really late here, and I've got this interview tomorrow. I'll let you know how it goes."

They said their goodbyes and after disconnecting Mark sat for a while, not wanting to turn around. When he did there was nobody there, of course. But Summerskill's book was lying open on the bedside table. Mark was almost sure he had left it closed. Almost.

He picked the book up, and noted that it was opened at the page with the scribbled note recommending the mysterious 'Gadabout '87'.

"What the hell?" he said.

It took him a few minutes online to find that Gadabout Press had been defunct since 1999. It had produced cheap paperbacks of out-of-copyright fiction, specializing in ghost stories. He found a second-hand copy of the Gadabout Dark Isle on eBay, but the asking price was steep. From the description, there was nothing special about the book except

42

that it contained 'Summerskill's last, unfinished tale, never before seen in print'.

"No way am I paying thirty bucks for that," he said to the empty room.

He waited a few moments, then laughed.

Like Montague Summerskill's ghost is telling me to buy a better edition of his book.

On a whim, he looked up the Wikipedia entry on Summerskill and found a head-and-shoulders photograph. It was blurred, probably clipped from a bigger picture. It showed a man with a clean-shaven face and a slightly mischievous expression in his eyes.

Mark opened his email account in another window and wrote a brief message to Sue.

'Hey, was this the guy you saw?'

He copied Summerskill's photo into the email, then hovered the cursor over Send.

Then he deleted the email.

***

"Thanks for coming, Mark," said Dylan Morgan. "I think we all appreciate that, in the circumstances, you would have been perfectly entitled to ask for this interview to be rescheduled."

The other two members of the panel expressed their agreement with Dylan, the chairman.

"Thank you for offering to postpone," replied Mark, "but as I said last week, I'd rather get it over with. Time is pressing for all people concerned."

"Very well," said Dylan, shuffling some papers. "Just so we're on the same page, we have funding for one visiting professorship here at St Caedmon's, and until now it's not been customary to offer it to the same person more than once. However, I think we can agree that Mark has put in an exemplary years' teaching, can we not?"

The other two panelists, John Wake and Moira Stewart, again made affirmative noises. Mark didn't know either of them well, but respected them as colleagues. Of the two, he felt

Moira might be more sympathetic, as Wake always struck him as a cold fish; an extreme example of British aloofness.

"Have they reached any conclusions about the fire?" asked Moira.

"Not that I know of," replied Mark. "But it seems the landlord hadn't done anything to upgrade the ancient wiring, and there were no smoke detectors."|

"The bugger broke a dozen laws, that's for sure," put in Dylan. "A tragedy; two young lives cut short, especially when both girls showed such promise."

Moira looked sidelong at Dylan and seemed like she was about to speak, then looked down at her agenda.

"Perhaps we should start, then?" asked Wake.

"Indeed," agreed Dylan, and the interview began.

Mark acquitted himself well, and the proposal for a paper about Summerskill did seem to impress Moira when he suggested it might generate some media interest. Wake was typically impassive, but did observe that favorable press coverage wouldn't be a bad thing in the circumstance. The conclusion was, as expected, that they had several other strong candidates to interview and Mark would be informed of their decision in due course. But he left the interview room feeling that he hadn't put a foot wrong.

Mark went to the college cafeteria, got a table, took out his phone and sent Sue another text, proposing a Skype conversation that evening. As he did so, another message arrived. It was an email, and something about it struck him as familiar. He recalled the morning he had met with Dylan to talk about Summerskill.

Yep, same thing, he thought, *just a link. Almost certainly a scam.*

Then he noticed that the mystery email was slightly different this time. Under the link was a simple phrase.

99 Days Were Allowed

He tried to delete the email but somehow bungled it and instead opened the link.

"Shit!" he said, angry at himself, then his eyes widened in

horror.

The image was that of someone cowering in a corner, making themselves small. He couldn't see the figure's face but the clothes and hairstyle were familiar. He was sure it was Katrina.

What kind of sick bastard would do this? he thought. *I should contact the police.*

But even as he watched the image flickered and faded, leaving his list of messages. The one he had just opened was nowhere to be seen.

"Could I have a word?"

Moira Stewart was standing over him, a laden tray in her hands.

"Of course! Please," he said, nodding at the seat opposite.

"Thanks," said Moira, sitting down and pouring herself a cup of tea from a tiny pot. "Is it bad news?"

"Oh, no, well, not exactly," he said, putting his phone away. "Some kind of glitch, maybe. Or I've started seeing things."

Moira smiled politely, clearly preoccupied. She seemed to reach a decision and asked,

"I hope I'm not speaking out of turn, but I did wonder if you had the whole picture. With regard to Katrina Lawless?"

Seeing his confusion she went on.

"Look, I hate campus gossip, but it's not exactly a secret that Dylan used to have quite a reputation for less than professional conduct, in regards to female students. You did know that?"

"I guess so," Mark replied. "But that was years ago, right? I mean, they were wild times in lots of ways."

Moira looked around, then leaned forward and lowered her voice.

"So we thought. But it may be that, in Katrina's case, Dylan reverted to his old ways, thought better of it, and then tried to keep her quiet with some sort of threat. At least, that's what one student counselor told me in strict confidence. I don't know how far things went, only that during her first year when he was her tutor, there was some kind of infatuation on her part."

"I had no idea," said Mark. "But what exactly is supposed to have happened? They had a sexual relationship?"

Moira shrugged.

"She never came forward with a specific claim, not officially at least. But there was a period, before you arrived, when her grades dropped disastrously and it looked as if she might have to leave. What I heard was he was persecuting her in some way, threatening her. Trying to get rid of a potential source of trouble. All that kept her from dropping out was Juliet."

Mark sat back, slightly punch-drunk at the thought that Dylan might not be the amiable old soak he had assumed.

"But come on, this can't have anything do with the fire!" he exclaimed. Heads turned at another table and he lowered his voice. "I mean, you're not suggesting that Dylan murdered two people? To avoid a scandal?"

Moira shook her head.

"No, of course not. This is really for your benefit, Mark. I think you're an excellent teacher but a bit naive. What I am saying is that Dylan's not really the amiable old boozer you might think. That image of the harmless dinosaur, a bit sexist, technophobe, coasting to retirement, is only half true. He's got a mean streak. Take it from me, I've seen him turn nasty without warning. You seem to be on his good side at the moment, but be careful."

***

"I still think you're reading an awful lot into a few old carvings," said Lucy.

She and Victor Carew were staffing the gift shop at the Abbey ruins, which doubled as the ticket office. So far, they had admitted precisely no visitors since opening at nine-thirty, two hours earlier, so they were occupying the time in their customary fashion- Bickering.

"Such skepticism," said Victor, "is hardly becoming in a young lady who owns a dream-catcher and takes homeopathic remedies. Why not check in your crystal ball if you want to know what the altar signifies?"

"Don't make this about me!" she riposted. "You're supposed to be the archaeologist, all scientific rigor. So where's the precedent for your amazing theory?"

Victor took a deep breath, but before he could reply, the door opened and their first visitors of the day came in. It was a party of Swedish pack-backers consisting of a middle-aged couple and their two teenage children. They were typically polite and serious, examining the contents of the small shop as earnestly as if it were the Tower of London or Buckingham Palace. They then spent a few moments calculating the exchange rate before deciding to pay for three bookmarks, a Skara Farne: Island of Mystery! A mug, and the Abbey tour.

As a volunteer, Lucy had the job of showing tour groups around while Victor guarded the shop's contents, most of which consisted of mugs, bookmarks, and cuddly toy monks. Sometimes, being a tour guide was a chore, but Lucy enjoyed talking to Scandinavians because they were so polite, interested, and usually spoke excellent English. This party proved no exception, asking sensible questions as she pointed out the remains of various monastery buildings.

"But why is it called the Red Abbey?" asked the daughter, who Lucy thought looked to be about sixteen. "I do not see anything red in the stones here."

"No, they are all gray," agreed the father earnestly.

Four pairs of blue eyes turned to Lucy, seeking enlightenment.

"That is true," replied Lucy, "the name refers to the blood that was shed here when the Vikings raided in the early ninth century."

"Vikings?" asked the father, frowning, perhaps anticipating a tirade against Scandinavians and their lawless antics. Or worse, jokes.

"Norwegian Vikings," Lucy added, hastily, "who sailed their long ships into Monks Bay one dark night and captured the monastery before the alarm could be sounded."

"And then they killed all the poor monks?" asked the mother, as serious as if they were discussing an atrocity on the evening news.

"Not at first," explained Lucy. "The monks had

considerable wealth in the form of gold crucifixes, silver chalices, and the like. That was all on display, of course. But the Vikings were convinced that there was more treasure hidden away. So they tortured the monks, including the abbot at the time."

"And was there any hidden treasure?" asked the boy, who looked to be two or three years younger than his sister.

"Sadly, no. The Vikings tortured and killed most of the monks for nothing, finally cutting their throats before throwing their corpses into the bay. After that, the raiders sailed away with their plunder, leaving the place in flames. It was rebuilt, of course, but from then on it was known to the locals as the Red Abbey, just as the bay is Monks Bay."

There was a brief pause as the four visitors absorbed the information, each in his or her own way. The parents looked suitably philosophical about man's inhumanity to man. The daughter looked personally offended, while her brother said something that sounded like 'Cool!'

"Did the Vikings ever come back?" asked the daughter.

"Yes, twelve years later, but this time, the locals were ready for them," explained Lucy, pointing north. "A beacon was built on the headland where that lighthouse stands today. Whenever a strange ship appeared, the beacon was lit, raising the alarm on the mainland so a shipload of warriors could be dispatched. After losing a couple of skirmishes, the Vikings soon learned to leave Skara Farne alone. Now, if you'll follow me, I'll show you a relic of Skara's most famous monk."

She turned and led the party to the base of the old altar.

"This," she said, "may look like just another slab of rock, but it is in fact all that's left of the private chapel of Abbot Thomas Beauclerc."

"Was this man a great English historical person?" asked the daughter.

"Aha, that depends on who you ask!" replied Lucy. "To some, he was a hero who preserved the monks during the time of the Great Plague, which as you probably know killed around one in four Europeans in the 14th century. But to others, he was a villain; a man who denied refuge on the island to the people from the mainland. Abbot Thomas is a shadowy, mysterious figure. All we can say for sure is that he was a man of great learning who ruled with an iron grip over the islanders, monks and fisher-folk alike."

The four visitors looked at the altar.

"Please, what do the carvings on this stone mean? They are not saints, I think?" asked the daughter, hunkering down to grab a picture with her phone.

"No, well spotted!" said Lucy. "For many years, people claimed they represented the four seasons. But my colleague, Victor, who you met briefly at the gift shop, he thinks they may in fact symbolize the four primal elements of ancient Greek science: Earth, air, fire, and water."

"Why would these pagan symbols be on an altar in a Christian building?" asked the father, frowning.

"Why indeed?" said Lucy. "But it may be related to the belief that Abbot Thomas had magical powers."

The only downside, she thought, *of people who are genuinely interested in this stuff is that I get out of my depth pretty quickly.*

"But practicing magic does not make sense if he was a monk, because that would be witchcraft," protested the daughter. All four members of the family looked at Lucy, clearly expecting her to clarify the matter. Again she felt the keen scrutiny of those blue eyes.

"Good point!" she said, playing for time. "The truth is that it's very hard to separate fact from folklore where Abbot Thomas is concerned. Locals claim he was a mighty warlock, but official church records merely list him as a very successful manager of a major monastic foundation."

The Swedes looked disappointed. The son, in particular, had clearly been expecting some more extreme violence.

The daughter squinted at her phone, then held it out for Lucy to see.

"Please, can you tell me why the carving is not visible in the photo?"

Lucy looked closely at the small screen. It did seem as if the panel in the image was blank. She looked down at the base of the altar. Of course the carving, showing the vague outline of what might be a flame, was there.

"Well," she said, "I think it might just be a problem with the camera not picking up a very faint image in this rather bright sunlight."

The others were now crouching around the square stone, all holding out their phones and exchanging Swedish chatter. A succession of bleeps and whirring sounds were followed by exclamations. One by one, they showed Lucy pictures of nothing but weathered stone, devoid of any images.

"This is perhaps the magic of Abbot Thomas?" asked the father, smiling. "Perhaps he does not approve of modern digital things?"

"Perhaps," Lucy replied, struggling to summon a smile of her own.

She ushered the family on to the remains of the monks' refectory, but found it hard to concentrate for the rest of the tour.

Chapter 4: Investigations

"First up," said Superintendent Masson, loosening his tie as Jo closed his office door behind her, "you owe me a favor. One day, perhaps when I'm long retired and a bit gaga and you're the first woman to run the Criminal Investigation Department, I'll call it in. From my luxury nursing home in the Algarve, with a bit of luck."

"Yes, sir," replied Jo Garland. She could tell from her boss's manner that he was going to deliver some bad news. She knew from experience that he was generally relaxed and rather pleased with himself when he did so.

Masson explained that his overseas contact had found nothing on Mark Stine.

"He's clean as a whistle," he said, with an air of disapproval. "One of those people who seem too good to be true, really. Not even a minor motoring offense back home in the States. Very disappointing, unless he's a secret agent and it's all part of a fake identity. Which isn't very likely, is it?"

"No, sir, not really," agreed Jo.

"So much for your hunches, eh, Garland?"

"Indeed, sir," repeated Jo. "Glad to have that cleared up, sir."

"Yes," said Masson, "but it's about the only thing that has been. How's the case been progressing, otherwise?"

Jo gave a summary of her team's results thus far. Despite expert scrutiny of the wiring, no evidence of an electrical fault had been found in the students' lodgings, so the cause of the fire remained mysterious. The landlord was hardly a model citizen. The man was facing prosecution for various safety code infringements. But it looked as if the fire had been a freak accident of an indeterminate nature and therefore, not the landlord's fault.

"In fact, one of the forensic guys suggested ..."

She paused, trying to gauge her superior's mood.

He's not going to like this, she thought, *however I dress it up.*

"Go on, is this another hunch?" Masson asked.

"Yes, but not one of mine. The term the fire investigator used was SHC," she replied.

Masson frowned.

"SHC? Is that another one of your modern techie terms from the internet?"

"Not really, sir," explained Jo. "It goes back a good few years. It stands for Spontaneous Human Combustion."

"Oh, I saw a documentary about that once, when I had to spend a week on the sofa with a slipped disc," said Masson, with an air of polite interest that didn't fool Jo. "I think it was part of a fascinating series that covered flying saucers, ghosts, and the yeti. Can't remember the exact name of the show, though. It was something like 'The Mysterious Baffling Unexplained World of Utter and Complete Bollocks.'"

"I know it's a fringe theory, sir," persisted Jo, "but the experts really have nothing else to go on. It's nothing like a regular house-fire, where it's almost always fumes that kill people over a period of a few minutes. Those girls seem to have died almost instantly, then various combustible stuff around them caught fire. It's as if something simply incinerated two healthy young people in an ordinary kitchen. Then the resulting heat triggered a relatively minor kitchen fire that was easily put out. There was plenty of smoke damage, but the only intense heat seems to have been limited to the victims. Their flesh was literally cooked on their bones, their clothes were burned to ashes."

Masson frowned again.

"So, sticking to the boring old facts the way we're supposed to, what we have are two dead people. Either they died in a freak accident, which covers spontaneous combustion, or they were victims of an impossible crime, for which we have no suspects. It's case closed, wouldn't you say?"

Jo began to speak, then paused.

"Go on, Detective Sergeant, since we're already in the Twilight Zone," he sighed, leaning back in his creaking chair and putting his hands behind his head.

"Well, sir, while the American lecturer may be in the clear, there is another possibility. We have someone with a possible motive."

She took a photo out of the dossier on her lap and handed it across the desk.

"So who's this smug-looking old git?" asked Masson, peering at the photo.

"Another member of the St. Caedmon's faculty, sir, one Dylan Morgan, Ph.D.," replied Jo. "He's their Senior Lecturer in English Literature and quite the ladies' man, according to a couple of former colleagues I managed to track down."

"At last! Something that makes sense to an ordinary copper," said Masson, leering at the photo. "So, Doctor Morgan, you're a dirty old man surrounded by youthful flesh in abundance, aren't you? And we all know what you intellectuals are like; randy little blighters. I blame Freud and D.H. Lawrence."

He handed the picture back to Jo.

"So he's got a motive strong enough for murder, you think?"

"Possibly. There's certainly evidence of serious wrongdoing on his part, sir," said Jo.

"Sex is one of the two classic motives for murder," said Masson, happy to be on familiar ground at last. "Sex-based crimes are at least as good as money-driven villainy, in my experience, and can be a lot more fun to investigate! Right, which of the victims was this Morgan bloke shagging?"

"Doctor Morgan was allegedly involved in a liaison," said Jo, choosing her words carefully, "with Katrina Lawless. It started about a year and a half ago, ended in the early months of this year. According to other students, she was very upset about it and almost lodged a formal complaint against him. But she was a rather timid, fragile personality and couldn't go through with it."

"Are we talking about allegations of sexual abuse here?" asked Masson, leaning forward.

"Possibly, sir, depending on your definition of abuse," said Jo carefully, "as the central issue here is power. He was her first-year tutor, responsible for her welfare. So any kind of physical relationship was off limits and he knew it. A career-destroying scandal could have deprived him of his current job and his pension."

"All right," conceded Masson, "but it's a bit of a reach to go from that to not only killing Katrina but a bystander as well, isn't it?"

"In a way, perhaps," said Jo, "except for one interesting point. This is not the first time this sort of thing has happened. Young women who get involved with Dylan Morgan seem to have nasty accidents."

That did the trick. For the first time since she had been assigned to Cambridge CID, Jo saw her boss's face break into a big, cheesy grin.

***

"What I need," explained Mark, "is an itinerary for this working vacation I'm planning. I was hoping you could help me work one out?"

Ralph Minns, Head Librarian at St Caedmon's College, looked enthusiastic. *But then*, thought Mark, *he always did*. A short, rotund, ginger-haired Scot with a bushy ginger beard, Minns was one of those people Mark thought had been born both middle-aged and absolutely sure of their life's purpose. In this case, the purpose was to convey all the collective knowledge of the library to anyone within range of Minns' voice, which was startlingly loud for a librarian.

"Itinerary? Ah, yes, Mark, I got your email! Happy to help!" he boomed, his voice echoing among the oak rafters of the beautiful 17th century building. Heads turned, but no-one could very well shush the boss. A few seasoned scholars at reading tables exchanged amused glances or rolled their eyes before returning to work.

"Follow me," said Minns, "I have the very thing."

He led Mark to his office, where he produced a series of photocopied sheets showing a series of handwritten pages.

"Extracts from Monty Summerskill's diary?" asked Mark.

"No, he didn't keep one," laughed Minns. "He was far too busy with lecturing, research, and administration. The man was a workaholic, especially by the standards of those more relaxed times. As well as collecting ancient manuscripts, he amassed lots of paintings and prints for the museum. No, these are Summerskill's letters to friends and relatives, notably his brother, who was a clergyman in Ireland at the time. Remarkably efficient postal service they had then, you know. Two collections and deliveries per day!"

"Fascinating," said Mark, politely. "But are the journals relevant to his fiction? I'm looking for accounts of the locations, folktales, and such like that inspired his stories."

"Oh, these are quite definitely relevant!" enthused Minns. "All these relate to his first cycling tour of Britain, in the summer of 1909, during which he got material for quite a few of his stories. He visited historic sites, archaeological digs, old churches, that sort of thing. I only wish I'd had time to actually draw a map of his route for you."

Mark skimmed through the sheets, frowning.

"I'm not sure I can decipher all of this," he said. "I'd have thought a guy living way before computers would have had much better handwriting."

"Yes, it is rather spidery, isn't it?" said Minns, cheerfully.

Mark shuddered, then looked more closely at the blotted, sprawling writing. There was something familiar about it.

"Hey, take a look at this, will you?" he asked, putting his bag on the desk and taking out *The Dark Isle*.

Mark opened the book and found the page with the faint, handwritten note on the blank page.

"Does that look like Summerskill's handwriting to you?"

Minns glanced at the book, then laughed.

"Yes, it does somewhat, but it's obviously a coincidence. After all, a man who died in 1916 could hardly write a message in a book published in, let's see, 1943, making a reference to a publisher active in 1987. Could he?"

"No, no! I just thought it was kind of amusing," said Mark, hastily.

What the hell was I thinking? Of course it's a coincidence.

"If I had to name a suspect for that intriguing message, I'd look no further than your friend Doctor Morgan," said Minns. "He's such an admirer of Summerskill and must have spent hours pouring over his collected letters. Quite clever of old Dylan, to suggest the ghost story author is commenting on his own book from beyond the grave!"

"It certainly is," replied Mark, perhaps too heartily. "Since we're on the subject though, is the Gadabout edition worth having? All I could find online is that it contains an unfinished story."

Minns sucked air through his teeth.

"Ah, yes! Several drafts of unfinished stories were found among Summerskill's papers," he said, holding up a finger like a magician about to produce a coin from behind Mark's ear. "I might be able to get my hands on them for you. Suppose you give me a couple of days to root around? So much of our stuff is still packed away in boxes. Ideally, it should all be digitized, of course, but there's nothing like the funding for that kind of project."

After years as an academic, Mark had become skilled at avoiding discussions of other people's budgetary issues. He made an excuse and left, but not before sincerely thanking the librarian for his help.

***

Lucy Hyde got up just before nine, after pulling a late shift at the pub the previous night. She breakfasted on oatmeal, whole-meal toast, and juice while looking out at the sea cliffs and, beyond them, the ever-changing complexion of Monks Bay. It was a view she could never get enough of; a daily confirmation that she had made the right decision by moving to Skara Farne.

At first, the only living things in sight were gulls and cormorants wheeling over the bay, which was dazzling under a cloudless sky. Then a lone figure appeared. She could tell at once from the stiff gait and the battered blue baseball cap that it was Sharkey, walking along the cliff path so close under the lighthouse he was barely visible from the small window.

What are you hoping to see out there, old man?

Sharkey had been walking the cliffs for a few days now, ever since the business with the phantom cyclist on the causeway. On impulse, Lucy changed into sweatpants, a tee-shirt and sneakers. By the time she got down to the door of the tower, Sharkey was almost out of sight, so she set off jogging after him. She liked to have an objective to make for in her morning run, and she felt the need to talk to someone.

Let's see if I can get more than a dozen words out of the grim old bugger today, she thought as she pounded along the cliff path. She took in great lungfuls of sea air, feeling the last traces of sleep leave her system.

Sharkey stopped and turned to look back and saw her.

He's got a sixth sense, Lucy thought. *Not the first time he's done that. Wonder what else he senses that I don't?*

By the time she reached the old man, he had turned away from her again and was looking out at the bay. Lucy followed his gaze and saw wheeling gulls and white-capped waves; the last vestiges of the small beach being taken by the tide. Then she saw something else, a sleek and shining form undulating across one of the flat rocks near the mouth of the inlet.

"A selkie," she said, shielding her eyes. "One of the folk of the sea. With the light dazzling your eyes, it's easy to see why tired sailors could see mermaids whereas we see rather tubby marine mammals."

"Bloody seals," returned Sharkey, gruff as ever. "Nothing magical about them, ask any fisherman! They'll pinch anything from a net, a line, or a lobster-pot."

"So what are you watching for, Sharkey, if not the local wildlife?" she asked.

Lucy thought she already knew. It was one of the things people talked about in the pub, using hushed tones. A local tragedy.

Sharkey turned and began to walk back the way he had come. *Back to his tumbledown cottage,* she thought, *and a solitude that's far worse than mine could ever be.* She fell in beside him, her long legs letting her easily keep pace.

"The spirits of the loved dead are never far away," she said. "Why look out there when they're always close at hand?"

Sharkey stopped for a moment, then continued walking without looking at her.

"People should mind their own bloody business!" he grunted.

"It's a small island," she said. "We all know everyone else's business."

"I don't need your help," Sharkey insisted, not breaking his stride. "Or your pity, lass!"

"You don't think you need it," she persisted. "But looking out there isn't going to do any good. That's not where they are, not now."

He stopped again, stared out over the bay.

"You think you know, but you don't. Wait until you lose everything, everyone you care about. Then you'll know."

Lucy was about to speak again when Sharkey's eyes widened in surprise.

Or is it fear? Some mixture of both? she wondered.

He turned and looked out at the bay again, shielding his eyes with a raised hand. Lucy followed suit, but couldn't make out anything unusual. Then she noticed the sound, the familiar mechanical drone of a light aircraft. A blurred dot became visible above the sea-dazzle.

"It's just someone on a sight-seeing tour, Sharkey," she said, "or maybe an RAF training flight."

He ignored her, continued to stare out over the sunlit waves. She was about to give up and resume her run when the plane appeared, flying in a great curving arc around the bay's northern headland. The seal on the rock disappeared into the water, emitting an oddly human-sounding cry of alarm. As the red and white aircraft grew closer, she could make out its unusual shape, a boat-like hull and small floats suspended from its wingtips.

Just a coincidence, Lucy thought. *Seaplanes aren't that unusual along this coast.*

Then the plane's engine stuttered, coughed, and resumed its throaty roar only to falter again. The propeller slowed, individual blades becoming visible. The aircraft wobbled, just skimming the flat rock. One of its wing-floats touched the water, then the wingtip itself went under. In a split second the plane was cartwheeling towards the shore like a toy that was flung by a piqued child. Fragments of wing and tail flew off while the fuselage vanished in an eruption of spray.

"No!" Lucy shouted.

"It's all right, lass," said the old man.

She realized she was gripping Sharkey's hand, and let go

58

with a mumbled apology. He gave no sign that he had heard her. Tears were streaming down his face. Lucy looked out at Monks Bay, and now she saw nothing but the restless waves. There was no trace of debris, no sign of any unusual disturbance.

"August 19th, 1982, in case they didn't tell you all the facts at the Grey Horse," said Sharkey. "My little girl, Shona, she wanted to go up in the plane. Adventurous spirit, like her mother. I told her that was just for the tourists, the price was too steep. But my missus, she said I was being a stingy old grump. So I paid for them both to have their flight round the island. Birthday treat, you see. She was nine."

"I'm so sorry," she said, laying a hand on his shoulder. The hand was shaking, she noticed, and he reached up and patted it.

"Don't be sorry, lass. At least I loved, and was loved. That's as much as most of us can hope for. No, worry about what's coming. Worry for us all."

"I don't understand," said Lucy. "Why torment yourself by coming out here, seeing this?"

For a self-style wise woman, I seem to spend a lot of time being baffled these days, she thought.

"I come here to see the crash because it's as close as I can get to them. Feeling the pain is better than feeling nothing at all," he said.

"Why the ghosts, why now?" she asked, looking him in the eyes.

"When the ghosts come back on Skara it's because something far worse is moving, something old and evil at work in the world," he said. "And the older the ghosts we see, the more things are being stirred up. You think you know about this island? No, lass. There are things on Skara that should be left alone, but people keep stirring them up."

"People?" she asked. "Who do you mean? What are they doing?"

"It's always the sort of people who are sometimes clever, but never wise. People who think they can use powers, or beings, that are best left alone. Fools!"

And with that last word, he walked off, head down, no

longer looking out to sea.

Sharkey had his vision, she thought. *Imagine having nothing but the love of the dead to give your life purpose.*

She left the old man to his memories and jogged back to the lighthouse by a different route. As she ran, she pondered Sharkey's warning, and wondered why it called to mind Victor Carew's theory about the mysterious altar stone at the Red Abbey.

***

"Tell me more!" said Masson, sitting bolt upright.

As she referred to her notes, Jo tried not to think of an elderly bloodhound suddenly getting the scene. Disrespectful of her boss. If rather funny.

"Back in 1994, Morgan's supposed to have had a pretty intense relationship with a student called Miranda Bell. She even went around claiming they'd become engaged and then told everyone who'd listen that he broke it off. Raised quite a stink and brought a formal accusation of sexual misconduct."

"Since he's still teaching, I assume this Miranda Bell withdrew her claim?" asked Masson.

"Not exactly, sir. A few weeks later, she went over a hotel balcony in Barcelona, fell six floors. A passing German tourist broke her fall. And his neck, as it happens."

"Ouch!" said Masson, with a touch of relish. "It would be too much to ask that Doctor Morgan was standing next to her on the balcony?"

"No, sorry, sir," replied Jo. "He was in Birmingham. He was working as a lecturer at the city university, while she was on holiday with friends. Quite a lively holiday, it seems. Booze, cannabis and a few tabs of Ecstasy were found in the room by the Spanish police, so they drew the obvious conclusions."

Masson stood up again and pondered the view of Cambridge.

"Right, so our friend, Morgan, avoids professional disaster by a narrow margin, thanks to an extremely convenient accident. What was the second case?"

"A very strange one, sir," said Jo. "A Ph.D. student named

Dolores Bayo. Very gifted, apparently, and Morgan was her tutor. This was shortly after he arrived in Cambridge. Back in 2001, she made allegations against him, lodged a formal complaint of sexual harassment. Then, a couple of days before the actual hearing was scheduled, Miss Bayo disappeared while out jogging in the woods around Grantchester. Her roommate reported her missing the following morning."

"Now that's more promising!" exclaimed Masson, turning round. "Did they find her?"

"Yes, sir, a man out walking his dog found Miss Bayo's body three days later. She'd been suffocated, according to the coroner's report, and then buried about eighteen inches deep. Definitely no accident this time. Those records haven't been digitized yet, sir, so I took the liberty."

Jo handed over some photocopied sheets, including scene-of-crime photos. Masson looked through them, tutted, and raised an eyebrow.

"Pity this was before my time," said Masson, "I was transferred here the following year. But if it had been a murder case I'd have certainly heard about it. So what happened?"

"They couldn't pin it on Morgan, or anyone else," explained Jo. "No forensic evidence, no witnesses, nothing. She was simply found in a shallow grave."

"But there must have been something," protested Masson. "Skin under her fingernails, for instance. Or fibers, hairs, if not actual DNA?"

Jo shook her head.

"Nothing like that, sir, just severe bruising where she'd apparently struggled against someone. Or something. One of the investigating officers said it was as if the ground had just swallowed her up."

Masson stared coldly at her.

"First, you suggest that two students spontaneously caught fire. Now it's what, homicidal forest pixies, killer elves?"

"I'm just reporting what was said, sir. I highlighted the relevant passage."

Masson frowned his way through several pages of the cold case report.

"So it seems you've got lots of data, a suspect, four corpses, and bugger all in the way of a case," grumbled Masson, perching on the edge of his desk to loom over Jo. She knew from experience this was his 'Go on, impress me!' posture, so she decided to play her best card.

"We do have a witness, in a way, sir."

"How so?" he asked.

"We only have three corpses, because Miranda Bell didn't die," she replied, trying not to sound triumphant. "I mean, technically she did, but they managed to get her onto a life support machine."

Masson gave a snort.

"I'm guessing she's not exactly a chatterbox after falling six floors, even if her fall was broken by some hapless German?"

"No, sir," Jo conceded, "Miranda Bell suffered severe brain damage and was in a persistent vegetative state for nearly eight years. But she's gradually shown signs of improvement and apparently, she can now communicate to some extent. Computer assisted, you know, a bit like Stephen Hawking. She can move one hand, a little. I had a long talk with her mother, who's her main carer."

"And you want to question Mrs. Bell's tragic daughter?" he asked. "At a rate of what, a word a minute?!"

Jo leaned forward, speaking rapidly.

"Sir, I know you don't think much of my hunches. But suppose this was your first case as lead officer and you had just come across a bunch of dead girls all linked to the same bloke, what would you do?!"

Masson gave a snort of laughter.

"You've got me figured out! Of course I'd start digging, and for the moment, Garland, I authorize you to do the same. Within reasonable limits. And try to keep your travel expenses down, for God's sake."

Jo nodded, shuffled her papers back into her folder, and got up to leave. But then she hesitated. Masson, ensconced once more behind his desk, sighed and said, "All right, Garland, you might as well tell me now. But if it's about the lost continent of Atlantis or something, you'd better have more than a hunch."

"I got some preliminary findings from the tech team, sir," she said. "They managed to recover the hard drives from both girls' computers, and found a lot of internet activity. Most of it was innocuous stuff, but there was a bit of action on some unusual sites."

Masson raised an eyebrow.

"We're not talking porn, are we?"

"No, sir," replied Jo. "It seems both girls were into Wicca in a big way."

After a pause, Masson asked, "I'm assuming it's got nothing to do with making that cane furniture everybody had in the Sixties?"

"No, sir," she said, barely suppressing a smile. "It's to do with traditional folk magic. Wiccans are people who think they're witches and warlocks. They tell fortunes, make charms, hold rituals. And sometimes they cast spells."

Masson stared at her for a long moment, then said, "Right, here's the plan. You put all this weird stuff into an email, send it to me, and I'll definitely read it ... at some point. In the near future."

"Yes, sir," said Jo, as she left.

Chapter 5: Encounters

"So, you're ready to embark on your pilgrimage, following in Monty Summerskill's bicycle tracks?" asked Dylan Morgan, tucking a napkin under his chin. They were in The Mitre, Dylan's favorite pub, for an informal chat.

"Yep, I've got my route mapped out," replied Mark. Over the last week, he had managed to work out a proper itinerary for his working vacation, one that would take him to various photogenic sites and furnish him with plenty of material for his blog. His academic paper on Summerskill would be more a matter of online research and old-style winging it, but he could do that anywhere with a Wi-Fi connection.

"Well, I'm glad it all worked out," said Dylan. "Nice to see young talent going full steam ahead."

"Thanks! Couldn't have done it without you," said Mark. "I'll be sure to mention you in the paper, or would you like to be listed as a co-author?"

"Good Lord, no!" replied Dylan. "All I did was make a suggestion, after all."

"How can you eat that stuff?" asked Mark, staring at the heaped plate of sausages and mashed potato in onion gravy that had just been deposited in front of his colleague.

"Pub grub, lad, can't beat it!" replied Dylan, putting down his pint of ale and picking up his cutlery. "You really should give bangers and mash a try, instead of nibbling that rabbit food!"

The Welshman gestured scornfully at Mark's salad with his fork before plunging it into a greasy 'banger', the omnipresent British pork sausage whose contents, Mark felt, were best left to the imagination. Not for the first time, he wondered at the national habit of using cutlery in such a genteel manner, no matter what you were actually eating. He looked around the lunchtime crowd and soon spotted a middle-aged woman attacking a burger with a knife and fork that she was holding like surgical instruments.

"I'll stick with the healthy option, thanks," he said, spearing a tomato, "you see, I was kind of chubby as a kid and it caused me a lot of grief in high school. So I got kind of compulsive about watching my weight. And yes, I am ready to begin my odyssey. It's taken a bit longer to organize, what with the inquests and all."

"God, yes, those poor girls," said Dylan, wolfing a mouthful of potato. Gravy stains were already accumulating on his napkin. "These slum landlords should be shot, charging exorbitant rents and putting young lives at risk."

"Yeah, I guess," said Mark, thinking back to his interview with the detective, Garland. He had got the distinct impression she suspected him of some involvement in his students' deaths. Then there was the bizarre email image, and Moira Stewart's warning. Was Dylan up to something? But if so, what could it be? Maybe it was all just down to campus rivalry and malicious gossip. He'd seen some pretty venomous feuds Stateside, no reason to think the Brits were any different.

"You look worried, old chap, anything else wrong?" asked Dylan.

"Oh, no, I've just lost a lot of sleep lately."

Mark decided not to mention his bizarre daydream about Billy Straker. He was determined to see it was a symptom of work-related stress, nothing more.

"Fresh air, good food, new experiences," declared Dylan. "That's my prescription for you, lad! Get out into the countryside, see something of England. Cambridge is all very well, but how much of the rest of this country have you seen? You're going stir-crazy, in a way."

He had a point. Apart from a few trips to London to see a show and do some shopping, Mark hadn't seen much of the country.

"You could be right," he said. "I'll certainly be seeing a lot more of little old England. I'm taking the train up to Lincolnshire, then going on to Yorkshire, and finally staying a few nights on Skara Farne."

"Ah, the Dark Isle itself!" said Dylan. "What did you think of that story?"

"I haven't gotten round to it, yet," admitted Mark. "But I've been quite impressed by the ones I have read."

"Only quite impressed?" Dylan stopped chewing, his fork

holding a chunk of sausage poised in mid-air. "Some of the finest examples of the traditional English ghost story and he's 'quite impressed'. I don't know. What a jaded lot your generation are."

"We've seen too many horror movies, I guess," conceded Mark. "But to get to the point, I'm just here to thank you for all your help. The journal accepted my proposal for a paper on Summerskill, so now all I have to do is write the damn thing."

"Wonderful!" exclaimed Dylan. "So pleased for you. When do you leave?"

"Blunt as ever," smiled Mark. "Couple of days, just have to finalize my hotel arrangements in York. I'm already booked into a B&B on Skara."

"Excellent, it's a lovely island, such splendid views," said Dylan.

"Oh, you've been there?"

"Just the once," replied Dylan. "And that was a long time ago."

"Oh, and that reminds me," said Mark, smiling, "By a stroke of luck, I managed to get a cheap paperback edition of Summerskill's stories, the one with the unfinished tale. It arrived this morning. So I can let you have your copy back."

Mark was already reaching down when Dylan dropped his fork with a clatter, sending fragments of gravy-soaked potato over the table.

"No, no," said Dylan, "don't think of it, old chap! You hang onto it for as long as you like."

Mark produced the battered hardback volume and laid it next to his plate.

Dylan stopped eating.

"I thought it might have some sentimental value?" he asked.

"Not at all! Really, keep it!"

Dylan was goggling at the old book as if it were a venomous snake. Then he caught Mark's eye and laughed.

"Hah, sorry!" he said, mopping at the mess of potato with his napkin, "It's just a rule I have. I never loan books, only give them as gifts. Much better that way! Loaning can lead to grief if books aren't returned. People fall out, friendships grow threadbare. You know the sort of thing, I mean?"

All the while his eyes kept darting between Mark's face and the Summerskill collection.

"Fine," said Mark, putting the book back into his bag. "That's very generous, thanks."

"Don't mention it!"

Shortly after, Dylan made an excuse and left. It was the first time Mark could remember his friend abandoning half a plateful of food and a nearly full pint of beer.

***

"She likes watching the wildlife shows," said June Bell. "I think David Attenborough's voice soothes her, as well as all the nice pictures, of course. Just so long as there's not too much violence. We tend to avoid the ones about the Serengeti."

Jo Garland followed the woman from the hall of the normal suburban house into what should have been the living room. It had been converted into a pristine, white-walled sick room where Miranda Bell lay. The thin figure in light blue pajamas was surrounded by what looked like enough hi-tech gadgetry to send a mission to Mars. The sound from the television almost drowned out an electronic beeping.

"Miranda?" said Mrs. Bell, turning down the TV volume, then leaning over to look into her daughter's face. "The police lady I told you about is here! Do you still feel able to talk to her for a few minutes?"

The thin, pale woman lying on the bed showed no sign of having heard her mother. But then Jo noticed Miranda's right hand twitch over a plastic pad lying on the covers. A second, smaller screen on a stand next to the bed came to life and two letters appeared.

OK

"Move into her line of sight so she can see as well as hear you," whispered Mrs. Bell to Jo, stepping back.

Jo sat on the single chair by the bed and leaned forward until she was looking into a curiously ageless face. Miranda

Bell might have been forty or fourteen. Jo had seen something similar in long-term prisoners. This woman's skin had been untouched by sunlight for over twenty years.

"Miranda, thank you for agreeing to talk to me."

Jo paused, then realized it was foolish to wait for the woman to make some inconsequential reply.

Imagine having to focus all your energy on just typing a word on a screen.

"Miranda, I wanted to ask you about Dylan Morgan."

After a moment, the woman's first and middle fingers began to move again, painfully selecting letters from an on-screen menu. Her response to Morgan's name was succinct, and expressive.

SHIT

Jo couldn't help smiling.

"Yes, I think so too, Miranda, but we've not been able to pin anything on him. Can you help me?"

This time there was no pause before the fingers moved.

TRIED TO KILL ME

"You're saying it was no accident?" asked Jo. "But the Spanish police report said that you fell off a balcony."

The beeping grew faster as the pale, pink-tinged fingers worked again. Jo tried not to stare at them. Miranda's eyes were a hesitant blue, the sort that's almost gray in artificial light. Jo could detect no sign of thought or feeling in them.

GUST WIND

"I don't understand. You're saying a gust of wind blew you off a balcony?"

Jo couldn't stop herself wondering if Miranda's brain damage had left her incapable of coherent thought, or at least prone to wild confabulation. Even at the best of times crime victims, like all witnesses, were notoriously unreliable.

YES, came the reply, then the baffling phrase IN BOOK.

"What was in the book, Miranda?"

CURSE

Jo leaned back, wondering if she had traveled halfway across England for no purpose. But she couldn't just give up. "You're saying Dylan Morgan put a curse on you?"

YES

"And this made you have your accident?"

YES

"Why did he do it?"

SHUT ME UP

Could it have been some form of hypnosis? wondered Jo, baffled by the turn the conversation had taken. *Perhaps the belief in a curse, some form of suggestion, might have led Miranda to jump off that balcony? But if Morgan could do that, why didn't he just order her to drop the allegations?*
The pale hand was moving again.

PAPER SYMBOLS

"Sorry, Miranda, I don't understand."
Jo was aware that the electronic beeping was becoming even more insistent. More words appeared as Miranda's fingers tapped the pad frantically, all the woman's personality seemingly concentrated into those two expressive digits.

FEARS GHOSTS BAD DREAMS

"I think that's enough," said Mrs. Bell, putting a hand on Jo's shoulder. "She gets tired quickly and becomes very frustrated. It's not good for her. Please, come and have a coffee."

"Thank you, Miranda," said Jo, "I didn't mean to upset you. I just want to get at the truth about what happened to you, and to some other people."

As she was leaving the room Jo glanced back at Miranda and saw a new word had formed on the small screen.

FOLLOWER

In the kitchen, Jo thanked Jane Bell, then tried to get the woman's perspective on her daughter's near-fatal fall.

"I'm convinced that that man, that Morgan person, had something to do with it!"

"Did you know that Miranda had a relationship with him?"

"Yes!" said Mrs. Bell. "She was so happy, at first. We, as in, my late husband and I, had our doubts, of course, because of the age gap, but we tried to be supportive. Then a shadow seemed to fall over her, she stopped calling as often."

"What kind of shadow? Was she depressed?" asked Jo.

"Not exactly," said Mrs. Bell. "No, it was more of anxiety. Once, Miranda said she felt she was never alone. I got the feeling there was a lot she wasn't telling us. That's why we were so happy when the shadow, whatever it was, seemed to lift and she agreed to go to Spain with her friends."

"She felt happier in the days leading up to her death?" asked Jo.

Mrs. Bell nodded.

"I don't know that there's anything I can add, except that I feel a bit ashamed of how we reacted at first, when we heard the news."

"How so?" asked Jo.

"Oh, I suppose we reacted the way any parents would have," said Mrs. Bell, "We were so angry with her college friends, because of the drinking and the drugs. I blamed them. When they told us that story about some kind of freak wind-storm that literally plucked Miranda off that balcony, we cut all ties with them. Never let any of them come and see her.

Well, you would, wouldn't you? But since she's regained some movement she's been insisting it was true, as you saw."

The woman looked into Jo's eyes, as if seeking some kind of definitive ruling.

"But it can't be true, can it?" the woman asked. "Nobody can conjure up the wind?"

"Logic says no," conceded Jo. "But there's a lot about this case that seems to defy logic."

After a few more minutes of inconsequential talk, Jo refused the offer of coffee, using the excuse of the long drive back to Cambridge. The truth was that the entire house felt like a hospital ward, everything clean and clinical and focused entirely on the woman kept alive by machines. Jo didn't like hospitals, and anyway she felt she had a wasted journey. There was no way she could go back to Masson with some story about a curse.

Jo had just started her car when it happened. The street was typical of the London suburbs, each house with a small front garden enclosed by neatly trimmed hedges. It was early afternoon, in the lull between school runs. A car alarm went off in the middle distance and Jo sighed.

Great, do I have to chase some kids away from a taxpayer's BMW, now?

She was wondering whether to ignore the alarm when another began its urgent mechanical protest, then within a few seconds, several more joined the chorus. Jo leaned forward over the wheel, peered down the avenue towards the growing racket. For a second, she thought she was seeing a bomb go off as a cloud of debris flew across the road. Then she realized that the neat garden hedges were being torn apart, seemingly by an invisible wind-storm heading up the street towards her.

A four-wheel drive parked about twenty yards ahead was rocked violently, setting off its alarm. Primal fear seized her. Something unknown was coming nearer, something dangerous. She reacted instinctively, flooring the accelerator and swerving into the middle of the road. Even then her Volvo was hit so hard by the invisible vortex that Jo thought she might have lost a recent filling. The hood and windscreen of the car was covered with leaves and other debris as the storm swerved into the Bells' garden. There was a series of crashes as wood and glass shattered.

Jo got out and ran towards what had been a neat semi-detached home. It now looked like a set for a post-apocalyptic movie, its door and big picture window smashed in. Jo shoved aside the garden gate, now dangling crazily on one hinge, and took out her phone to call in the emergency. She was so shaken she forgot the house number as she made her way into the hall, then looked down and saw it on the front door she was standing on.

A terrible wailing sound began. June Bell, her face streaked with blood oozing through a layer of white plaster dust, was clambering over wrecked furniture into the front room. Jo followed, already knowing what she would find. The air was thick with dust and where Miranda's bed had been was what remained of the ceiling.

***

That night Mark found himself oddly unwilling to go on reading the Summerskill book. A distaste he couldn't understand came over him every time he picked it up. But even he couldn't bluff a proposal for a serious paper on a book he had not actually finished. So he flipped to the table of contents and plumped for the second shortest tale.

'My Sister's Dolls' House' seemed an innocuous enough title.

Probably a nice bit of Old English whimsy about childhood toys, he thought. *Nostalgia in flatulent prose, bound to send me to sleep.*

The story certainly began in soporific fashion, with several paragraphs of reminiscence about an idyllic childhood in a small English village, where the narrator's father was a much-loved parish priest.

> *My dear little sister, Emily, was never in good health, and spent much of her time confined to a bedroom or nursery. She was of course somewhat spoiled as a result, being allowed toys that might have been denied*

a girl who could enjoy the healthy pleasures of the great outdoors. Of her many splendid toys, Emily had a favorite, a magnificent dolls' house of, I believe, French manufacture, complete with splendid appurtenances that recalled Versailles. It was the gift of a grateful parishioner, an elderly lady who had resided for some years in Paris during the last century and had been, it was rumored, somewhat less than virtuous.

Mark smiled at the suggestion, familiar from so much British and indeed American fiction, that anything involving the French must be morally dubious. He switched on his tablet computer and started making notes. At first, the story seemed pleasant enough, as Emily naturally names the dolls after herself, her protective older brother, and other members of the family. The narrator, despite a very 'manly aversion to dolls and such-like girlish delights', allows himself to be roped into Emily's pretend tea parties, hunt balls and the like, 'much to the amusement of the gardener's boy, whose ears I had to box for his impertinence'.

So far, so humdrum. But as Mark read on, the story took a darker turn, and the sunny nostalgia turned to bitter reminiscence. The narrator, evidently recollecting events in old age, described how he returned home from university to find that 'Emily, who had just attained the age of twenty-one and was finally beginning to bloom after so many years an invalid, was resolved to marry a man utterly unworthy of her'. A whirlwind romance had taken place, apparently, with a rich man who had moved to the neighborhood only a few months earlier.

Mark duly made a note about the fact that, until she attained the so-called 'age of majority', a woman in those days needed her father's or guardian's permission to marry. But as he tapped out the brief sentence, he felt a growing unease with the direction the story was taking. He had the impression that he knew what was going to happen next, and that it was something very bad.

Sure enough, a couple more paragraphs on the word

appeared. The unnamed narrator meets Emily's fiancé and is repelled by the man's 'mean, stooped, almost hunchbacked frame, and his way of walking, almost scuttling'. As was almost routine at the time, deformity or disability is equated with moral depravity, and Emily's betrothed has a 'sneaking, venomous character'. All this prompts the narrator to give the man a nickname; *The Spider*.

Mark paused, unwilling to keep reading.

I know this story.

He must have read it as a boy in some anthology of ghost stories. It was probably one of those cheap paperbacks that were handed around at school, with titles like *A Hundred Tales of Terror* or *Stories to Scare You Stiff*. Mark knew what came next, and it had given him nightmares for weeks. He had already had a mild case of arachnophobia, no biggie, but then Summerskill's story had turned it into a raging psychosis. His younger self had forgotten the author's name, the story's title, even the basics of the plot. But the imagery had remained rooted in his subconscious like a poisonous weed.

"Aw, come on, Stine, you're a grown man!" he said aloud. "Get a grip!"

The sound of his voice only seemed to emphasize that he was alone. The small bedroom, which normally seemed quiet and cozy, now seemed awfully silent. He lay there, simply listening, becoming aware of the blood rushing in his ears, the sound of a distant siren coming through the half-open window. Was there something else? A scratching sound?

No, don't be ridiculous! You've just had a stressful time. You need to focus and get back in the zone.

He read on, turning the page, bracing himself for the few dozen words that had deprived him of so much sleep. Yes, he remembered more details now, like the moment when the narrator receives a tear-stained letter from his father telling him that Emily has died, apparently of a 'wasting disease, as if the very life had been sucked from her'. The Spider leaves the neighborhood after the funeral and is never heard from again. After Emily's funeral the narrator, emotionally shattered, finds himself in their childhood nursery and sees the once-beautiful dolls' house in the corner, now sadly neglected. He looks in through windows half-obscured with cobwebs, and sees the Emily-doll lying on the dusty carpet of the splendid hallway.

Here it comes. I've got to read this, right to the end.

On top of the doll is 'a huge spider, far larger than those commonly found even in rural houses, its legs wrapped around the head and shoulders of the hapless figure, its bloated body quivering gently, as if in the throes of ecstasy'. The narrator recoils in horror, then 'burns the doll-house and all its contents on the garden rubbish heap'. But this fails to exorcise the horror that 'haunts his dreams to this very day'.

You and me both, pal, thought Mark.

The scratching sound began again, louder this time. Mark thought of the ivy-covered walls of the old college buildings, and what a good purchase all the foliage would provide for something that was already pretty good at climbing. Something with too many legs.

I won't sleep tonight, he thought, and got up to do some more work on his proposed paper. But before he started, he closed the window and drew the curtains. Then he made some instant coffee of the usual British standard, which was terrible but something he had had to get used to. After an hour or so, he was absorbed in his proposal and feeling good about it, but he was also feeling the effects of several cups of coffee.

Oooh boy, I've really gotta pee.

One of the drawbacks of having temporary lodgings in a medieval building designed to accommodate students was that he had to share bathroom facilities, as if he were in a youth hostel. It was another thing Mark had gotten used to after the first few weeks at Cambridge, but tonight, walking the few yards along the corridor daunted him. The vast majority of students had left for the long summer vacation, leaving the block unnaturally quiet.

God, he thought, as he opened his apartment door, *what I wouldn't give for the sound of drunken singing wafting up the stairwell right now.*

He flicked on the low-powered lights and made his way to the bathroom. It was better lit, but its stark, utilitarian look gave it an institutional feel.

Not reassuring, he thought. *Like being in a better class of*

jail. Urinating proved difficult in his state of heightened
nervousness. The situation wasn't helped by the scratching
sound of what must be ivy at the window.

*Must be windy out there. Strange, it was calm enough
earlier.*

Then something hit the window, hard. Mark spun around
and glimpsed at what looked like a long, crooked tree-branch
waving outside the pebbled glass. His heart was pounding,
now. The branch disappeared.

"Don't be so childish," he said firmly to his reflection as he
washed his hands, then went back to his room.

It was only later that Mark remembered the only tree in
the courtyard was nowhere near the bathroom window. He
struggled to rationalize what he had apparently seen and
heard. Eventually, he snatched a few hours of sleep just after
five, while the eastern sky grew bright with a new dawn.

Chapter 6: Visions

"A trick of the light," said Victor Carew.

But he didn't sound convinced by his own argument.

"Come on, Victor," said Lucy, "you took a rubbing from those images only the other day. But a digital camera, several cameras in fact, can't record them. How is that?"

She held up her own phone, scrolled through four images of the facets of the altar stone. Each showed a blank rectangle.

"Trick of the light," he repeated. "And if that's not a good explanation, what is?"

Ignoring him, she asked, "Can I have a look at your rubbings?"

Victor held up his hands in mock surprise.

"But this is all so sudden! Shouldn't we at least try dinner and a movie first?"

Lucy waited, arms folded, for him to finish his comedy routine. Innuendo was part of their working relationship, and so lacking in any genuine sexism that she had formed the opinion Victor was that rare specimen, a gay man who wasn't yet willing to come out.

"Finished?" she asked when he stopped and ran out of innuendo for a moment. "Those rubbings are the best images of the altar carvings we have, so I thought I'd see if there's anything similar to be found online."

Victor duly produced his sheets of tracing paper and Lucy scanned them into the PC in the shop's back office. She then managed to get online and uploaded the scans onto an image-finding site. It generated a few hits. The first few examples seemed to be coincidental, down to the eroded vagueness of the carvings. But the fourth was pay dirt.

"Come and see this, Victor!"

He came and saw, then gave a low whistle.

"Well, score one for the digital age," he said. "I'd never have thought to look there, but with hindsight it's so obvious."

The match was with the Skara Book of Hours, a priceless medieval book kept at the British Library in London. It had been created on the island in the 14th century during the time of the Black Death, under the supervision of Abbot Thomas Beauclerc. It was an illuminated manuscript, hand-decorated with beautiful and often quirky works of art by monkish scribes. And one of the illustration towards the end of the volume, contained the odd symbols found on the altar stone.

"I don't recall seeing that particular illustration before," said Victor, leaning in closer to scrutinize the small image. "But that does seem to be the symbol for fire."

Lucy agreed. The symbol was a detail in a picture covering an entire page. It showed a man, evidently meant to be a wealthy merchant judging from the table in front of him, which was laden with documents, a set of scales, and heaps of gold coins.

"Business is not going well, it seems," observed Victor.

The merchant was recoiling in exaggerated horror from a streamer or banner that was draped across the table.

"I think that's part of the earth symbol," said Lucy, pointing. "It's half-hidden by a fold of that strip of cloth or whatever it is."

"Yes," agreed Victor, "so maybe all four elements are represented on it. But what is it? A scroll of some kind?"

"Well, I once reacted like that to a scarf I got for Christmas."

"Frivolous child," he said, "look at the legend above."

There were a few faded words running along the top of the page, not in English.

"Can't read 'em," she said, "except maybe that one. Maledroit, is it?"

"Malediction," corrected Victor. "Medieval Latin, meaning a curse."

Lucy looked again at the horrified merchant.

"He must have short-changed the wrong person, then."

Victor didn't respond for a moment. Then he pointed to the window behind the merchant, which showed a typical medieval artist's landscape of stylized hills and trees.

"What do you think those other figures are?"

She could just make out a hooded figure on a hill, evidently a monk.

"I can only see one," she said. "No, wait, now I've got him!

78

Or it."

The other figure was only vaguely human in shape, a black silhouette halfway down the hill. It was crouching or perhaps loping across the valley towards the cursed merchant. Something about it repelled Lucy. The medieval artist had somehow conveyed a sense of menace by a simple outline.

"I suppose it could be symbolic of the plague striking down the rich and worldly?" she said.

"Possibly," said Victor. "But that piece of cloth or parchment, what can its significance be?"

"No clue," admitted Lucy. "But our merchant certainly knew what it was. It's telling him his number's up."

Victor agreed. The anonymous, long-dead monk had done an excellent job of capturing the man's fear, confusion, and despair.

***

Mark opted to travel by train, as Montague Summerkill had done, along with his trusty bicycle. Mark hadn't ridden a bike since he was twelve and had no intention of starting again. Instead, he planned to take cabs to most of the destinations he needed to visit, and then hire a car in Newcastle to drive up to Skara Farne for a long weekend.

On the first stage of his odyssey, Mark opted for the so-called 'quiet coach', a concept that always amused him seeing how reluctant Brits were to talk to anyone on trains at the best of times. The idea was that you said nothing above a whisper, didn't play any music or videos, and ideally kept any typing you did nice and quiet, too. No frantic keyboard-bashing allowed!

It was a good working environment, especially as Mark had struck lucky and the carriage was almost empty. In fact he could only make out one other passenger, or at least the top of someone's head over the back of a seat at the far end.

As the train pulled out of Cambridge he got started on his blog. He entitled his first post: WORKIN' ON THE RAILROAD!

He then typed,

'I'm off! Heading north on the first day of a working vacation, following the route of the celebrated British ghost story author Montague Summerskill.'

After a few more paragraphs, Mark added links to sites on Summerskill, then ended with,

'Follow my supernatural adventures in the weeks to come!'

Then he uploaded a picture of Summerskill and then hit Publish.

There, he thought. *I'm committed. I've finally started this so I've got to finish it. And that means finishing the goddamn book!*

He took out his copy of *The Dark Isle* and turned to the title story. It began with some scene-setting as Summerskill's hero, a 'gentleman and scholar at Cambridge' called Mister Bright, has been working too hard and is told to get away from it all by his doctor. He asks around for the quietest possible holiday venues and eventually settles up the island of the title, a 'place of wave-worn granite cliffs off the North Sea coast'.

So far, so predictable, thought Mark. *But I'm guessing he finds it less than relaxing when he arrives.*

Sure enough, when Bright crosses the causeway to the Dark Isle on his 'trusty bicycle' he finds the locals less than welcoming. Shockingly, he finds it impossible to recruit an island woman to 'come in and do' for him, which Mark felt reasonably sure meant cooking and cleaning. A trip to the local tavern leads to the usual icy silence when Bright walks in. Bright consoles himself that 'this aversion to strangers will at least allow me plenty of time for reading, walking, and solitary contemplation.'

Summerskill's leisurely prose coupled with the rhythm of the train in the quiet carriage made it hard for Mark to keep his eyes open. Lost sleep caught up with him, and he found himself dozing.

"Real pretty country. Everything's so green."

Billy Straker was sitting opposite him, looking out at the landscape rolling past. The bullet hole in his forehead wasn't bleeding any more, and the stains on his shirt had dried to a disgusting brown. Billy's skin had changed color, too, turning a kind of gray-green. Mark guessed that his long-dead friend had moved on from freshly-slain to the early stages of decomposition.

"This isn't real. I'm dreaming," he said.

Billy looked around, a thin smile twisting up the ends of his mouth. His lips were bloodless, stiff, the smile more of a facial spasm.

"Maybe! Not for me to say, Markie boy," said the corpse. "I'm just along for the ride. Like I said, ghosts are getting stirred up all around you."

"I must have dozed off. When I wake up, you'll be gone."

"Could be," conceded Billy. "Point is, here we are, so we might as well catch up, the way old friends do, huh?"

The dead teenager put his elbows on the table, leaned closer. Mark could see the whites of Billy's eyes, only they weren't so much white as a mess of yellowed tissue and broken blood vessels.

"So, when I asked if I could crash at your place that night, did you even think before you said No and hung up?"

"I didn't owe you anything!" said Mark. "You got yourself in trouble!"

Billy nodded, smiled again.

"Nobody's denying that, Markie. I was in way too deep, paid the price. Two in the body, one in the head."

Mark frowned.

"You said three in the body last time!" he pointed out, oddly satisfied at catching out his dream-tormentor.

"Did I?" Billy lifted his blood-stiffened shirt and looked at his torso. There were three bullet holes. "Sorry! Hard to keep count when you're being murdered, you know?"

"I'm sorry you died, Billy," said Mark.

"Well, that's something," replied the corpse. "Not quite the eulogy I'd have wanted, but then you never made it to my funeral, did you?"

"You were a good friend in high school," Mark continued. "I might not have made it without you."

With that admission, all Mark's worst memories welled up. He had been the fat, nerdy kid who made a nice, big target for all the bullies. His shame at being victimized had been almost as bad as his terror that, if he went home too messed up, his mom would notice and go to the principal. The chances of Brenda turning up drunk and yelling abuse were just too high to risk it. So he had tried to hide the damage as best he could. When she was conscious, Brenda was usually so drunk, she was unlikely to spot anything less serious than a broken limb.

"Remember that one time I ran into you outside Wal-Mart, and Brenda totally came on to me?" asked Billy. "Lord, you were blushing so hard I could have toasted marshmallows on your face, man!"

"My mother was an alcoholic," Mark replied, feeling all the old anger at his mother surge up. "She never took responsibility, never tried to get control of her life. She even died in a stupid accident, just walked straight out under a truck."

"Hey, something I've been meaning to ask, why'd she make you call her Brenda?" asked Billy.

"You already know!" retorted Mark, angrily. "You're a figment of my imagination, by definition you know everything I know."

"Maybe," said Billy, giving another rictus smile, "but maybe I'm a real ghost. Ever think of that, Markie?"

Billy nodded to the Summerskill book, opened on the small table between them.

"You read all that supernatural crap, teach students all about its social significance and stuff. But you've never taken a moment to ask, what if it's true? That maybe people believe in ghosts because we're as real as anything else?"

"Okay," sighed Mark, "we'll play this game by your rules for now. Until I wake up. So I called my mother Brenda because she hated me calling her Mom. It made her feel old, and it reminded her she'd had me because she was just too drunk to take her pill at the right time and then didn't realize she was pregnant from a one-night stand at a motel until it was too late for an abortion."

Once Mark had begun unburdening himself, he found he couldn't stop.

"'You're the biggest mistake of my life, Markie,' she would tell me any day she had a problem, which was most days. That was her refrain. That was what I usually got in place of a bedtime story. My drunken mom telling me I was her biggest mistake. And she made a lot of mistakes before that last one."

"You see?" said Billy. "You never told me all that stuff. Okay, I could've guessed a lot of it, but maybe if you had spilled your guts every now and then it would have been – what do you smart guys call it? Cathartic, that the right word?"

"You know it is," snarled Mark. "You were always a lot smarter than you made out. The dumb jock thing was mostly an act."

Again the smile came, but this time the lips barely moved.

"Yeah, you got me," said Billy. "I figured it didn't pay to seem too smart in high school. Only thing you're allowed to be real good at is sports, right? But you never got that. I mean, you were kind of a genius, but that's the one thing that never occurred to that big brain. To act a little dumb."

Billy leaned forward.

"And now you're being dumb! You're missing something else, Markie, something important, a matter of life and death. If you don't wise up, pretty damn soon the Follower's gonna kill you. The answer's in the book, Markie boy! Just not where you're looking!"

Mark started to ask what Billy meant, but then blackness rushed in through the carriage window and a sudden roar silenced him. He jolted upright, and the train emerged from the tunnel. The seat opposite was empty, of course.

***

"Here," said Masson, putting a glass in front of Jo. "Get that down you."

Without thinking, she picked up the glass, downed half its contents, then started to splutter, face reddening. It had been nearly four hours since she had watched a team of firefighters take the body of Miranda Bell out of the ruins of her home, three hours since she' ha left the distraught June Bell in the care of her police counterparts in London.

"Christ, what is this stuff, Sir?" she asked.

"That, young lady, is the most expensive brandy they have in this grotty pub. Talk about rank ingratitude!" he replied, taking a mouthful of his pint. "Brandy is supposed to steady the nerves, anyway, so get it down you. Your first actual death, was it?"

She nodded, then shook her head, still confused.

"No. There was this homeless bloke, when I was on regular beat work back in Liverpool. I found him under a bridge down by the canal. He'd been dead a while."

Masson nodded.

"Had the rats been at him?"

Jo nodded, shuddering at the memory.

"Yeah, saw a few of those in my time," sighed Masson. "But this is a bit different, isn't it? Someone you've just been talking to, so you can put a name to a face."

Jo took another swig of the brandy.

"I just don't understand it, sir," she said. "It was like a tank came along the street, then a bomb hit the front of the house."

Masson nodded.

"I've been talking to some contacts in London, nothing formal. According to them, five security cameras, all motion-triggered, all filmed the incident from five different angles. And they all recorded nothing except hedgerows being ripped apart and cars getting bashed about. On the face of it, what happened is impossible."

He shook his head.

"They've found no evidence of explosives at the Bells' house," he went on, "at least that's something. No hint of a terrorist connection. We don't want Special Branch and MI5 trampling all over our case. Things are messy enough already."

For a few moments neither officer spoke. The pub, part of a soulless national franchise, played a steady stream of 'classic' pop. A disco track ended to be replaced by the Stones singing

'Sympathy for the Devil'.

"What do you think really happened, Jo?" he asked.

She looked up, face still warm from the alcohol, and said, "Sir, I think that freak windstorm that nearly killed Miranda Bell in Spain came back and finished the job."

He didn't react as she had expected. There was no snort of derision, no pitying look. Instead, he took another mouthful of beer, then said, "I can't put that in a report, even if I believe you. And some part of me does. But, for the sake of argument, why come back for her now? Why not at any time in all the years she was a cabbage?"

Jo made a helpless gesture. The question had been bothering her.

"Best I can think, sir, is that my asking her about it somehow, I dunno, drew its attention. Triggered it again. She used the word 'Follower' to describe whatever this destructive force is. Maybe it doesn't want to be known, talked about, too widely. Before I turned up, the only person she had communicated with was her mother."

"That's quite a theory," he said, noncommittally. "A destructive force that can't be seen, or stopped? Perhaps not even understood? That's way above my pay grade, never mind yours."

Jo leaned forward, lowered her voice.

"When I started at CID, somebody told me not to expect everything in a case to make sense. It's not like on the telly, he said. The killer doesn't always have a nice, neat motive. The alibi that sounds ridiculous might be rock-solid truth. And when things don't make sense, the best you can do is stick to the hard evidence you've got, and follow leads wherever they might lead you."

Masson smiled at that.

"He was a right know-it-all, whoever he was. But he was right. We've got three dead students, and all linked to this Morgan bloke. Have another go at him, do some digging. But first, finish your brandy, then go home to Terry, switch off, forget about work. Get some sleep."

Jo, a wine drinker, struggled with the spirit while Masson finished his pint of real ale in silence. Then, as they were about to leave, he asked,

"Oh, I read your report on Wicca. Amazing stuff, and not in a good way. You really think those girls were looking online for ways to stop a curse?"

"Yes, sir," she said, gathering up her things. "Either that, or they were trying to find a way of deflecting it onto someone else, or maybe bouncing it back at the one who cursed them."

"Do I need three guesses as to who that might be?" asked Masson, pulling on his jacket.

"No, sir," she replied.

'Sympathy for the Devil' ended. As they were leaving the pub, Jo heard the first chords of the Doors' 'Light My Fire'.

Chapter 7: A Feeling of Unease

Mark's overnight stay in Lincoln brought no more visits from Billy Straker. This should have been a relief. But Mark found it difficult to relax in the unfamiliar English city. He had developed the odd sensation that he was being watched. On a couple of occasions, he even spun around in the street, convinced that someone was standing right behind him. Yet both times the nearest person was several yards away.

Then there was the incident at the Cathedral, which was featured in one of Summerskill's stories, 'The Wraith'. There was an admission charge, and the young woman at the ticket desk seemed puzzled when Mark asked for just one ticket. She leaned sideways to look behind him, then shook her head in good-natured puzzlement.

"Sorry," she said, "I thought there was someone with you for a moment."

The Cathedral itself was interesting but after taking a few pictures, Mark felt the urge to get back to his room and do some work. Again, he felt that odd sense of someone close on his heels as he made his way through the streets of the medieval city. When he entered the hotel foyer the automatic doors hesitated, started to close behind him, opened fully again, then finally closed. Mark went past the elevators and took the stairs to the second floor, telling himself he needed the exercise.

Back in his room he made some coffee and re-read Summerskill's story. Set in mid-Victorian times, 'The Wraith' offered a detailed description of the cathedral during a chill winter when an ill-advised bishop decides to have an old, unmarked tomb torn out to make way for various improvements. Disturbing the tomb releases a demonic entity that wreaks havoc among the clergy and choirboys. It was one of Summerskill's more predictable tales, but effective thanks to atmospheric writing.

I'd better include some of that on the blog, thought Mark, as he fired up his laptop.

But before he began a new entry, he checked for reactions

to the previous day's entry, the one made from the train. He was a little disappointed to note that only one person had commented. It was Sebastian from his tutorial group and had the student's usual slightly mocking tone.

'Nice pic! Who's your friend?'

Mark frowned, scrolled up to look at the blog entry. The only picture was the selfie he had taken just after getting on the train, and at first he couldn't see what Sebastian was referring to. Then he looked more closely at what he had assumed to be a shadow behind his seat. If you made a slight effort, you could see the shadow as a hunched figure looming over Mark. He could almost make out a rudimentary face, consisting of two dark eye sockets and a gaping mouth.

No! That's garbage!

He slammed his laptop shut and stood up and started pacing. All the strange and disturbing events that had occurred over the last few weeks were churned up in his memory. Things had been going so well for him, with only the Sue situation causing him any worries. Then, out of the blue, he had started having weird dreams and feeling insecure.

It can't be overwork, I've never felt like this before.

Mark sat down in front of the mirror and looked at his face. He had lost weight as well as sleep. He had a haunted expression. His eyes were tired and his cheeks were hollow.

This was supposed to be a vacation. A time to unwind, recharge my batteries.

Yet nothing had really happened. Or rather, nothing had happened to him that a psychiatrist wouldn't diagnose as symptoms of stress. The shock of two students, people he had gotten to know and like, dying suddenly and in a horrible manner might well be enough to explain it all. His subconscious was playing tricks on him, turning normal doubts and concerns into the stuff of the ghost stories he studied and taught.

Yeah, that's the rational explanation.

But it didn't convince him at a deep, visceral level. Instead, he reflected on what Billy Straker had told him.

He said the answers in the book. What could that mean?

He picked up the Summerskill edition that Morgan had given him and scrutinized it. He turned it over in his hands, studying the battered, faded green boards of the cover as if they might contain some clue. Then he peered at the blank pages, noted again the scribbled comment about the Gadabout edition.

Then it occurred to him.

Did this all start after Dylan gave me the book? Maybe.

But again, there was a logical explanation. His subconscious had focused all his anxieties about his career, about remaining in Cambridge, upon the gift from his friend. Then the terrible accident that killed Juliet and Katrina had unsettled him even more, and the result was –

"Craziness," he told his reflection. "I may actually go crazy if I don't snap out of this."

He opened his laptop again and reacted to Sebastian's comment.

'Ha! Yes, one of Monty Summerskill's ghosts, no doubt!'

Then he wrote a new blog entry about Lincoln and its cathedral, uploading a couple of photos of the latter. He wanted to include a short passage from 'The Wraith'. The Gadabout paperback was lighter than Dylan's old copy, so he propped the book up in front of him and started to type.

'Bishop Fawley's decision to have the unmarked tomb removed was considered unwise by many, but the prelate was a man who brooked no argument. However, a few days after the offending stonework was torn out and the rubble carted away, the bishop began to feel oddly out of sorts. If he had been asked he would have been hard put to describe his affliction. But in his journal he describes it as 'a feeling of unease, of never being properly alone; nothing more precise than that.'

Mark stopped typing.

Do I feel 'properly alone'?

The honest answer was 'no.'

He had a definite sensation of being watched. It made no sense, but there it was.

Right, do I need to go to see a shrink?

The alternative was to accept that the paranormal was real.

So how does a guy tell the difference between a genuine supernatural phenomenon, like a ghost, and a hallucination? Maybe if somebody else sees it too?

So far, people had seen two 'ghosts' associated with Mark. Sue had reacted to what might have been Monty Summerskill haunting his old college rooms, and now there was the shadowy figure on his blog.

Yeah, right, because nobody's ever faked anything supernatural on the internet before.

Both could be clever pranks by a student or just some random hacker. No, he needed something more substantial.

Billy said to look in the book.

He picked up the Gadabout paperback, then put it next to the book he had been given by Dylan Morgan. The thought occurred to him.

I've been thinking about something written in the book, like the scribbled note at the back. But maybe it's a physical object inside it?

He picked up the old hardback and instead of opening it, he held it so that he could look along its spine. As usual, there was a small gap between the glued mass of pages and the stiff cloth of the spine proper. The space was too small to conceal anything substantial. Then he ran a finger along the spine. There was a slight lump about a third of the way down. It was almost imperceptible. Almost.

You could hide something very small in that gap if you shoved it down with a knife or something.

"To hell with it, it's my book now," he said, and ripped off the spine.

A small cloud of dust arose, making him sneeze. For a moment, he thought he had ruined the old book for nothing. But then he noticed a pale pellet lying on the hotel room desk. At first he thought it might be a lump of old chewing gum secreted many years ago, but when he picked it up, the texture revealed it to be paper.

Rice-paper, in fact, he thought.

Afraid to tear the thin paper, he took his time teasing the pellet open. After several painstaking minutes, it proved to be a rectangular slip about an inch wide and four inches long. On it were four symbols that Mark had never seen before. They were in red and black ink, clearly handwritten, and he got the impression that someone had taken a lot of trouble getting the details just right.

But what do they mean?

He turned on the desk lamp and held up the paper, studied the symbols. Each consisted of a stylized image in a square frame. One was almost certainly a flame, another seemed to be some kind of winged creature, while the third consisted of a wave-like symbol. The fourth was vaguely familiar, a cross inside a circle. What they were doing inside the book Dylan Morgan had given him, Mark couldn't begin with guess.

***

"Doctor Morgan?"

Jo Garland stood uncertainly on the deck of the narrow boat, wondering if she had the right vessel and whether you were supposed to knock on a door if it happens to be in a floating home. A large cat lay on the roof of the cabin, observing her with mild interest.

"Hey, puss!" said Jo, extending a hand to just a few inches in front of the animal's nose. The cat accepted the overture, stood up, and rubbed its head against her knuckles.

"Making new friends!"

She turned to see Morgan standing on the riverside path.

"Always so difficult, especially for someone in your line of work, I'd imagine," he said

Morgan made the small leap onto the deck with surprising grace.

Like a fat old tabby cat that can still hunt, Jo thought.

"I'm sorry to bother you," she began, ignoring his

comment.

He raised a deprecatory hand.

"No bother, Detective Sergeant, always pleasant to receive visitors. Please, come in!"

He edged past her on the small deck and she tried not to recoil too obviously. There was something oily about Morgan, she thought, a too-obvious attempt to be a charming, intellectual eccentric. He unlocked the cabin and ducked inside, followed by the cat, then Jo.

The first time she had talked to Morgan had been in the formal context of his office at St Caedmon's. He was now on summer leave, and she had been directed to his unlikely home by the college authorities. It was conventional wisdom that you didn't interview someone on their own territory if you could avoid it. Any experienced officer knew it was better to bring them into the station and throw them off guard. But Jo had no real grounds to suspect Morgan of anything.

Except, she thought, *of being a sleazy old bastard.*

"Can I offer you some tea, or coffee?" asked Morgan, clattering around in the small galley.

"No, thank you, sir, I'd just like to follow up on our first discussion."

"Ah, yes," said the academic, "do take a seat, if you can find one."

Jo looked around and saw the cat already curled up on the only seat that wasn't covered with books and papers. She moved carefully along the dim-lit cabin and stood at the entrance to the galley, blocking Morgan's exit. It was a small move in a power game, her way of taking the initiative.

"I'd rather not take up too much of your time, sir," she said, "I just wanted to ask if you had anything to add to your remarks about Katrina Lawless?"

Morgan didn't look up from the kettle, which was coming to the boil.

"I think I told you everything pertinent to your investigation, Sergeant," he replied.

"Detective Sergeant," she corrected. "And you said that your relationship with Miss Lawless was entirely professional at all times?"

The kettle boiled, switched itself off with a sharp click. Morgan lifted it and poured boiling water into a mug.

Carrying on with his domestic routine, Jo thought, *totally unfazed.*

"As I said, she was a fascinating and intelligent student and her death is a great loss."

"And you didn't have sex with her at any time?" asked Jo. "Maybe you have it off with so many of your students you forget a few faces, names, other parts?"

Morgan lifted the tea bag from the mug and flung it casually into a garbage bin under the tiny galley sink. He still didn't meet Jo's eye.

"I did not," he said, "and I'm surprised a police officer would give credence to campus gossip."

"Do you remember Sylvia Bayo?" she asked, determined to knock him off balance.

Morgan took a bottle of milk out of a small refrigerator.

"I do. Another brilliant student. Lovely girl, a great loss. Her poor family."

He poured a dash of milk into the tea, turning it from black to murky brown.

"They never caught the maniac who killed her, did they?"

"I had an interesting chat with Miranda Bell the other day," she said.

This time Morgan did look surprised.

"She's still alive?" he stammered. "I thought – I mean, I assumed she must have died by now, but of course they can do amazing things these days."

"She is dead, now," said Jo, keen to keep him off balance, "though her name hasn't been released to the press yet. She was killed in some kind of freak windstorm a few minutes after she told me you wanted her dead. Quite a coincidence, don't you think?"

Now Morgan looked genuinely confused, angry, but not intimidated.

"That's absurd!" he snapped. "I happen to have taught some young women who, through no fault of mine, met with tragic accidents."

As quickly as it flared up, Morgan's anger vanished and he

was all smooth charm again.

"Do forgive me, I must admit the thought of that poor girl quite upset me. How she must have suffered!"

His smile made her want to punch him.

Short of saying 'I killed them and you can't pin a thing on me' he couldn't be more obvious, she thought.

"Miranda said you did it, and I believe her," she said quietly, leaning into the galley. "And if I ever figure out how you did it, you'll wish you'd never been born."

Morgan picked up his mug and took a sip of tea.

"My dear girl, you are clearly upset," he said. "I'd recommend a little rest and recuperation. Far away from me."

"Threatening a police officer is a criminal offense," said Jo.

"I merely offer advice," he said. "It befits the elderly, like myself, to give wise counsel to the young."

"It's not wise counsel that's the problem," she replied. "It's abuse of power and worse."

"Be careful what you accuse people of," said Morgan.

He moved close to Jo, well inside her personal space. She could smell beer on his breath.

"I wouldn't want your promising career to be cut short merely due to a few reckless remarks."

Chapter 8: North

"Ghosts?" asked Victor.

"Yes," replied Lucy.

The friends in the middle of what had become a summer evening ritual, chatting over mugs of chamomile tea in Lucy's garden at the very top of the lighthouse. The huge revolving arc-light had been removed when the building was decommissioned, so Lucy had turned the glassed-in space into a circular greenhouse. It proved to be an inspired choice, as everything she planted thrived. All of the plants she grew had medicinal purposes. Almost all were legal.

"You've been seeing ghosts?" asked Victor, looking as if he expected her to reply with 'No, only joking!'

"Not just me," she pointed out. "Sharkey as well."

Victor's expression showed that he didn't rate Sharkey's endorsement of the supernatural very highly.

"Come on," she pleaded, "all that stuff with the altar stone is real enough, isn't it? We've got four Swedish witnesses. That must be some sort of acid test for reliability."

"Yes, we've got an unexplained phenomenon," he pointed out. "That doesn't mean we can just dive into the paranormal and accept, well, any old nonsense. I mean, if Sharkey told me he'd seen a yeti running across the causeway, I wouldn't necessarily believe him."

"I know what I saw out in the bay," she retorted. "And it can't just be a coincidence. Strange things are happening here, and maybe in other places too."

Victor raised a questioning eyebrow.

"Do tell, my dear."

Lucy explained that she had noticed some chatter on Wiccan sites about a supposed curse that had killed two students in Cambridge. It seemed that one of the students had been asking online about Skara Farne and Abbot Thomas. About curses, and how to counter them."

"Coincidence, surely?" said Victor. But he looked uncertain.

"Remember the abbot's reputation for being able to curse

people, bring down some sort of supernatural vengeance on his foes?" she asked. "Suppose whatever powers he had could be revived, harnessed by someone today?"

Victor stood up and looked out over Monk's Bay, beautiful in the summer sunset.

"Medieval chronicles are full of miracles, curses, angels, and demons. People didn't separate fact from fantasy in those days, especially when the fantasy was popular."

"Sounds like you're trying to convince yourself," said Lucy, joining him at the railing that circled the lamp gallery.

"All right," he said, "let's assume there's a link between the symbols on the altar stone, your curse that's exciting the Wiccan world, and ghosts."

He looked at her with a smile.

"I can't believe I'm talking about this stuff as if it were as real as, well, death or taxes! I was such a fan of The X-Files when I was your age, now it seems I'm living in an episode."

Lucy, smiling back, said, "I've seen that show. You'll notice that in a lot of episodes the heroic FBI agents fail to stop a whole bunch of innocent people from getting killed?"

"Thanks for pointing that out," he said, ruefully. "But, assuming we're the heroes in this scenario, what exactly can we do? Report Abbot Thomas to the police for doing evil, occult things without a license?"

"No," she said, "but we could do some detective work, try to find out how the pieces fit together. We've already got some clues. If I do more digging online, could you check the archive in the fort?"

"Oh, I hate that place!" exclaimed Victor. "So dank and run down. But, if it will please you, I will start digging first thing tomorrow."

"Good! We'll swap notes when I come in to work on Friday."

He didn't reply, instead leaning over the rail to stare at something that was evidently near the base of the lighthouse.

"Careful, Victor! That might not be safe," she warned.

"Sorry," he said, standing upright. "What were you saying?"

"That we'll do some research and compare notes on

Friday? At work?"

"Right," he said, still distracted.

"What's so interesting down there?"

"Someone walking past," he said. "Hard to tell from directly above, of course. But I'd swear they were dressed in the robes of a medieval monk."

Lucy looked into Victor's face, trying to find a hint of his typical capricious humor. But he seemed deadly serious.

***

Just get on with it, though Mark. *What else can I do?*

The phrase had become his mantra as he continued his journey to the north. He kept dutifully making notes and writing blog entries over the course of a busy week. He posted pictures along with his thoughts on the various locations, but took no more selfies. After Lincoln, he had visited York, then moved on to the Cathedral city of Durham. The ghost or dream of Billy Straker had not returned since he had found the slip of paper. And he could always ask Dylan Morgan about it when he got back to Cambridge.

Mark still had the disturbing sensation of never being alone, but forced himself not to think about it and tried to keep busy. The next time he Skyped with Sue he tried to sound optimistic. After all, he had plenty to be positive about. But she knew him too well to be taken in.

"Mark, what's wrong?" she asked. "You've been preoccupied for weeks, now. And you've lost weight. Are you even eating properly? We've talked about this! I know how you get when you're fixated on some project."

For a moment, he was tempted to tell her everything, then realized how crazy he would sound.

You see, honey, there was this kid at school called Billy Straker and he was kind of a jock and somehow he got to be my best pal. Then when we left, we kind of drifted apart and he got in trouble and then he was murdered. And now he's come back as a ghost to warn me that I'm in danger from some kind of paranormal entity.

"Oh, it's nothing, hon," he said to the screen, "I just have trouble sleeping in hotels. And eating in them isn't exactly a joy, either. It's the best diet plan, believe me."

She didn't look amused by his attempt at humor, and he braced himself for more questions. But she surprised him by changing the subject.

"Anyways, I booked my flight! I'll be with you at the end of July!"

"That's great!" he replied, wishing he could sound more enthusiastic. "What's the exact date?"

Sue told him and he tried to enter it in his laptop's calendar. But for some reason, the computer refused to let him input anything on the date concerned.

"Aw, this thing's not playing ball. Anyway, send me all the details so I can meet you at the airport," he said.

They chatted some more before signing off. As soon as the conversation ended, he tried to input the date of Sue's arrival into his phone. But here, too, the calendar refused to accept the information.

Weird coincidence, he thought.

Dismissing the glitches, he lay down on the bed and took out the Gadabout paperback of *The Dark Isle.* He had read all of Montague Summerskill's tales apart from the title story, and resolved to get it done now. He would be arriving at Skara Farne soon, and should have the author's take on the island fresh in his mind. He opened the book and began to read, but as before Summerskill's opening paragraphs were not particularly gripping. Mark almost nodded off until the story's hero, the 'eminent folklore expert, Professor Bisley' got his first glimpse of his destination.

I rounded a headland and saw, to the north, a truly impressive vista. A great island girded by wave-washed cliffs, lay perhaps a mile or so off the coast. Its most impressive feature was a fortress dating from the various wars against the Scots in Tudor times, which stands on the island's highest point. The remains of the Red Abbey were not visible, being low-lying and overgrown.

Mark read on as Bisley crosses the causeway to the island,

arrives at the village inn and starts poking around. The locals prove friendly enough until the curious scholar starts asking about Abbot Thomas, a medieval monk reputed to have had magical powers. Everybody clams up, of course. The landlord of the inn tells him that 'folk round here don't talk about the abbot', who apparently resented people prying into his murky affairs when he was alive, and still does so in death. 'Just talking about him brings bad luck, or worse', warns the landlord. So Bisley goes to the old fortress, now a private residence, and asks the owner if he has any books about the mysterious Abbot. The helpful gentleman, who takes no interest in local folklore but has inherited an impressive library, produces a centuries-old volume that he describes as 'a lot of superstitious nonsense' but of some potential interest.

Cut to Bisley in his room at the inn, examining the borrowed book. He discovers that two pages have been glued together, separates them, and finds two pages of Medieval Latin, 'perhaps the work of the mysterious Abbott Thomas himself'. The text appears to be 'a spell for summoning someone or something', and the narrator says it aloud, 'rolling the quaint syllables around my mouth'.

Guess what, thought Mark, *he's inadvertently raised the ghost of the mean old abbot.*

Sure enough, Summerskill's narrator finds himself haunted by a figure in a hooded robe, which he tells himself is a figment of his imagination. The islanders become even more wary of him, and his host at the inn tells him that there's been a mix-up over bookings and he must leave at once. The narrator decides to go but then a terrible storm comes out of nowhere and makes the causeway impassable. None of the fisherman will take him back to the mainland in a boat, treating him as 'a veritable Jonah'.

"Come on Monty, land the plane," said Mark growing impatient. The story so far was too long-winded for his taste, all atmosphere and no real ideas.

Things took a more promising turn as Bisley resolves to confront Abbot Thomas 'with proper Christian fortitude', clutching a crucifix while reciting the Lord's Prayer. But Summerskill implies that his character's faith is too shallow to provide an effective shield against evil, thanks to Bisley's 'modern, intellectual' temperament. Sure enough, the next time Bisley walk around a corner to see the hooded figure standing there, he can't do anything but panic and run back to the inn. As he flees, he is followed by 'mocking laughter that echoed along the narrow village lane'.

In the final paragraph, Bisley is sitting at his desk studying the old book in the hope it will provide him with some kind of a get out clause when he hears 'a rustling, not unlike that of the hem of a robe or cloak being dragged across a carpet', and then he feels a hand upon his shoulder. Turning his head, he sees 'in the flickering lamplight a span of skeletal fingers like the legs of some unimaginable spider–'

"Oh, great, thanks Monty," exclaimed Mark.

The room suddenly seemed a degree or two colder. He forced himself to read on, about the spectral fingers clutching Bisley's shoulder. Fingers 'almost devoid of flesh, yet still animated by some force that allowed them to tighten their grip so that the yellowed fingernails began to cut into the fabric of his smoking-jacket'.

Kind of a weak ending, after all that build-up, thought Mark, laying the book down. *Unless you're an arachnophobe. The old bastard must have thrown that reference in knowing it would creep some readers out. What a sadist!*

Mark wondered why Dylan Morgan had praised the book so highly when the long title story was nothing special. Sure, there was enough material in the book for a decent paper, and the blogging was going okay. He had been careful not to over-stress the weird circumstances of Summerskill's death, but had hinted at it just enough to stir up some non-academic interest. With luck, it might even lead to some attention from the media.

He had to admit, Dylan had come up with a good career move for Mark.

So why don't I feel grateful to my best friend in this entire country?

Shrugging off the thought, he picked up the paperback again and flipped through to the last item, which according to the book's editor was supposedly a 'short draft of a story found among the papers of the author after his death'. It consisted of a few disjointed paragraphs that made little sense to Mark.

Weird kind of story, he thought. *More like a first draft of a letter that was never sent. But Summerskill uses the epistolary form elsewhere, so that's not so strange I guess.*

After a while, he gave up trying to puzzle them out, and drifted off to sleep fully dressed.

***

After her unpleasant conversation with Morgan, Jo Garland decided to take an evening stroll through Cambridge to get some fresh air and regain her composure. Her first impulse had been to call Masson and tell her boss, *I'm sure the bastard killed them all. He came this close to boasting that he had.* But then he would have asked her how Morgan committed murder, and that would have left her floundering.

She walked through the center of town, barely noticing the crowds of tourists and summer school students who were starting to throng the pubs and restaurants. Then she saw a face she knew, one with a link to the case. Yes, it was that student, Sebastian Wilde, who had shared the student house with the fire victims. On impulse, she crossed the narrow street and intercepted the young man.

"Mr. Wilde? Detective Sergeant Garland, you remember we talked about the fire?"

The student looked at her blankly for a moment, then she saw recognition in his eyes.

"Oh, yes, of course. Was there something else you wanted? I thought I'd given a clear enough statement."

"It was fine," she reassured him, "but that's not what I wanted to know. Walk with me? Somewhere a bit less noisy?"

They made their way down a side-alley to a small churchyard.

"I take it this isn't a formal interview?" asked Sebastian, as they sat on a bench amid the tombstones.

"Not at all," she said. "I just wanted to ask about Dylan Morgan."

"Ah, the aging Casanova," snorted the student. "He's

notorious, but the university authorities prefer to look the other way. And he's been lucky so far, I suppose."

"But Katrina Lawless could have changed all that?" asked Jo.

"Possibly," he conceded, "if she'd had the guts to complain officially. That's what Juliet wanted her to do. But I think, if I'm honest, that Katrina was so confused and frightened that she didn't know what to do."

"What was she frightened of?" asked Jo.

"I never could work that out," he admitted. "It's not as if old Dylan's the violent type. Nobody's ever suggested he knocks his women about. But he did have some hold over Katrina, and it made Juliet furious. They never discussed it with me, always stopped talking when I walked in on one their intense discussions. But ..."

Sebastian paused, and for the first time looked uncomfortable.

"What is it?" she asked.

"I didn't remember immediately after the fire. I was so upset, confused, you know?"

She nodded impatiently.

"Look, I did overhear them talking about burning something," he said.

"Do you mean starting a fire?" Jo asked.

"Christ, no!" he said, "it was nothing like that! No, it was just that Katrina said something to Juliet like 'I should never have burned it'."

"Burned what?"

"No idea," admitted Sebastian, "like I said, whenever I walked in, they clammed up. Didn't trust me, obviously. But there was one thing that happened a few days after they mentioned burning ..."

He paused, and Jo nodded encouragingly.

"Look, it's silly, but one morning, the girls asked me for a favor. Juliet, really, as Katrina was always unwilling to speak up for herself. It was very simple, but for some reason, I got the impression it was a big deal for them."

"So what was this favor?" asked Jo.

"Well, that's the absurd thing," he said. "All they wanted

me to do was return a book that Morgan had loaned Katrina. They'd been at the book loaning stage for a few months, before they progressed to less intellectual pleasures. I suppose that was part of the old fart's technique. Obviously, Katrina never wanted to see him again, but I suppose she was too honest to simply keep the book or chuck it away."

Jo felt disappointment. This didn't seem to be leading anywhere.

"What sort of book was it?" she asked.

"Oh, just some boring old ghost stories," he replied. "Not even on the English syllabus, just some bilge from the glory days of the Empire. That's what was strange, the way they asked me, and then handed this tatty old book over, it felt like it was a bomb or something. It made me wonder. If anyone else had asked me, I'd have suspected a practical joke, you know?"

"So you took a good look at this book, first chance you got?" asked Jo.

He smiled, slightly shamefaced.

"I admit, I looked through it on the bus to college that morning, hoping there was something out of the ordinary. Maybe some kind of tacky dedication from him to her, written inside, you know? But there was nothing special about it. Cheap edition, worse for wear. Worth about five pounds. Not much of a lover's gift."

"And what did Morgan say when you gave it back to him?"

Sebastian thought for a moment.

"Actually, that was a little odd too, come to think of it. I went to his study first thing and he was just rolling in, still not quite sobered up. So I just pulled the book out of my bag and said, 'I believe this is yours, Doctor Morgan?' He took it, mumbled something, and was just going into his study when he stopped. He looked at the book, then at me, did a sort of double take. It was comical! Then he opened the book and riffled through it the way I had, only not out of idle curiosity. He did it in a sort of frantic way, as if he was afraid he'd find something."

Sebastian paused.

"So, what happened next?" asked Jo.

"Oh, that was it," replied the student. "I guess he didn't find anything in the book, either. It's just his reaction that seems odd, in retrospect. After Morgan examined it more closely he looked relieved, and then he gave a sort of embarrassed laugh. Then he just thanked me and went inside his study without another word."

"Any idea why?" asked Jo.

"Maybe he was expecting a death threat!" said Sebastian, laughing as he stood up. "Look, I've got to go. But if you can pin something on Morgan, good luck to you."

"One more question," she said, getting up. "Mark Stine, the American lecturer? He's a good friend of Morgan's?"

"In a way," the young man said. "Stine's a nice enough bloke, and he certainly knows his stuff, but he's so wrapped up in his work that he can't see what's right under his nose."

"Like Morgan's unethical conduct with female students?"

"Among other things," said Sebastian. "Truly selfish people like Morgan don't really have friends. Just people they use."

He left Jo mulling over another piece of a chaotic puzzle.

If in doubt, do routine police work, she thought. *So next on my to-do list to talk is the bright but unworldly Mark Stine.*

Chapter 9: Connections

Mark woke up just after midnight, struggling his way up out of a nightmare. The dream faded almost instantly, leaving him with its mental aftertaste.

Something was chasing me. Something with more legs than anything ought to have.

His mouth was parched and he decided to get a drink of water, then have a shower. He undressed and put on a robe, then went into the small bathroom. When he clicked on the light, the man he saw in the mirror was a thinner, hollow-eyed version of the Mark Stine he knew. He filled a glass with water, then turned off the faucet. The sudden absence of noise seemed oppressive.

There was a scratching noise. It came from inside the glass shower cubicle behind him. In the mirror, he saw a sudden movement and the scratching sound came again, louder and somehow more insistent. Menacing.

Mark turned to look at the shower cubicle. Though frosted glass blurred his view of the interior, he could still make out the shape of a vast spider, a creature with legs as long as his arms and a bloated body bigger than a football. His turning seemed to trigger the monster's predatory instinct and it began to scrabble fiercely at the cubicle's door.

He screamed, lost it, rushed out of the bathroom and then tore open the door of his room, desperate to escape. He was stopped by a jerk on the belt of his robe. He had been caught.

"No!" he whimpered, and hurled himself out into the corridor.

"Blimey, I didn't realize it was that sort of hotel!" said a high-pitched voice.

Mark looked around to see a party of three young women standing at the end of the short corridor. They were dressed for a night out that was evidently coming to an unexpectedly entertaining end.

"Not bad," said a second woman, "but we didn't order a stripper!"

This produced a chorus of giggling and shoving. The trio

showed no inclination to move on, so Mark held his robe closed with one hand while he recovered the belt from the door handle.

"Sorry," he mumbled.

He started to go back into his room, but couldn't bring himself to cross the threshold.

"Hey, he doesn't look well. Are you all right, pal?"

The woman who had spoken first, walked up to him, looked into the room.

"Is somebody giving you grief?" she asked.

"Jealous husband, I reckon!" shouted one of her friends, causing another burst of giggling.

"Shut up!" shouted the first girl. "He's obviously had a shock."

She walked past Mark, leaving traces of perfume and booze in the air, and pushed the door of his room wide open.

"Be careful!" he shouted, dismayed to hear his voice break in panic.

"Oh!" said the woman, and looked around with a smile. Then she reached over and took Mark's hand.

"Look, none of my business," she went on, "but running around naked, screaming and shouting in the middle of the night isn't going to solve your problems. You two boys need to have a good talk."

Then she walked off, none too steadily, to join her friends who had vanished out of sight, though Mark could still hear their laughter.

"Shut it, you two!" she called after them. "Have a bit of decorum."

"What was that all about anyway, Kirsty?"

"I reckon it was just a lovers' tiff. How come the best-looking ones are always gay?"

Mark stared after her as she disappeared around the corner leaving him baffled by the exchange. Then he looked into his room again, and saw Billy sitting in the corner, next to the television.

"Come on in, Markie," said Billy. "Third time's the charm!"

Mark came in, seeing no alternative.

"She saw you? I mean, that girl out there, she could see you?"

Billy was looking normal for a dead person. His football shirt was unstained, his face unmarred by an entry wound.

"Yeah," nodded the ghost, "some people do. Kids, if they're imaginative, and kind of lonely. And adults who've been through a lot, maybe gotten damaged in the old noggin. Or in that particular little lady's case, they spend a lot of time close to death."

Mark's puzzlement prompted Billy to give his old, full-throated laugh.

"Those were a bunch of overworked nurses unwinding on a night out, Markie! Taking a well-earned break from the splendid British National Health Service."

Mark was baffled.

"How could you tell? They could've been anybody."

Billy laughed.

"Take it from me, I can just tell. You get to know these things when you're dead! Kind of compensates for stuff like not having a pulse."

Mark sat down on the bed.

"You don't look as half as dead as you did last time," he pointed out.

Billy stood up and looked in the mirror above the desk.

"Thanks! Yeah, I'm looking a lot better. That could be because it's my last visit. Gotta make it classy!"

"You only get to talk to me three times? Why?"

Billy shrugged.

"Well, why not? Three's just a classic number, like with wishes and stuff. Little pigs. Bears that make porridge. Hey, I didn't invent the rules! Still got no idea who did, to be honest. Earthbound spirits don't know squat about the Big Picture, it seems. Point is, you know about the curse now, so what are you gonna do about it?"

It was Mark's turn to shrug.

"The curse is that slip of paper?"

"Yep," said Billy. "And whatever you do, don't lose it!"

"But what do I do with it?" asked Mark.

Billy wagged a reproving finger while shaking his head.

"Oooh no, I can't just tell you! Remember what I said about rules? It's only because you're a special case that I'm allowed to help you at all."

"I'm a special case? What do you mean?" demanded Mark.

Billy shrugged.

"Hey, all I know is I get to turn up three times, tell you some real important stuff, then poof! I'm outta here for good. Off to the astral plane, Nirvana, maybe even heaven with fluffy clouds and everybody playing harps in birkenstocks. But I digress! First time I warned you, second time I gave you the clue, now I'm telling you one last thing. So listen up, buddy!"

"Well?" asked Mark.

Billy spoke two words, and then vanished.

***

"Find anything interesting?" asked Victor, as he unlocked the Red Abbey gift shop.

"Age before beauty!" countered Lucy.

"Very well," he sighed. "I poked about in the archives and found a few books on island folklore. Some of them talk about the curse that Abbot Thomas placed on those who displeased him. And there's something interesting in one of them, something a bit more specific."

He lifted a shopping bag.

"Right," she said, following him inside. "I'll get the coffee brewing, you turn everything else on, and we can compare notes."

Five minutes later, they sat in the office studying a dog-eared book.

"Half of the pages have come unglued," Lucy observed.

"Not unlike my brain after a night spent reading this stuff," said Victor. "But this is interesting."

Lucy tried to spell out the faded text on a stained, torn page, then gave up.

"My medieval Latin isn't that great, sorry."

"Obviously," said Victor triumphantly, "as it is in fact written medieval French, the language of the ruling class in Abbot Thomas's day. What it says is simply this. 'Certain marks made on paper, empowered by an incantation, have the power to draw from the dark regions' a 'Persecutor'. Or perhaps the modern equivalent is 'A Follower', the translation is tricky. Anyway, whatever the mysterious being is, it says it 'will pursue, torment, and eventually destroy he who possesses the paper at the appointed hour'."

"That seems a bit of an elaborate way to commit suicide," objected Lucy. "Why not just chuck yourself off a cliff?"

"Ah, that's the clever bit!" he said. "It goes on, 'if another person willingly accepts the cursed paper, then the entity will destroy him within the designated time, which is five-score days less one'. Or ninety-nine days, in plain English."

Lucy nodded thoughtfully.

"Take a look at this," she said, logging on to the office computer. "This was something I found, a link to on a Wiccan site talking about the fire that killed those students."

She soon found a YouTube video of a black-and-white British cinema newsreel from 1914. It was entitled 'Quaint Customs on Skara Farne'. Folk ritual.

"I didn't know there were any customs," said Victor, "apart from the Saturday night lock-in at the Grey Horse."

"Watch," ordered Lucy, "this custom died out shortly after. And I think I know why."

The grainy, jerky footage was just a couple of minutes long. The picture was almost lost in a blizzard of faults on the negative. But it was still possible to glimpse what was going on.

A group of islanders were gathered in the village square where the war memorial now stood. Victor noted that the people were evidently dressed up for some kind of carnival, the men in suits and ties, the women in bonnets. People were buying food from a fish and chip stand, there were smiles and general merriment.

"Watch!" said Lucy. "This isn't just a public holiday. This is a ritual."

An inter-title appeared on screen.

THE ABBOT!

A robed, hooded figure stood slightly apart from the revelers. It might have been a statue draped in a monk's habit until it raised an arm. The Abbot's finger pointed at the crowd, which parted as another oddly-costumed figure appeared. Again the film cut to an inter-title. This one read,

THE CURSED!

The Cursed was a young man with a whitened face, dressed in rags and wearing a woolen fisherman's cap. He was skulking and trying to hide behind various locals, all of whom pushed him away and into the center of the square. Who he was trying to avoid became clear when a second bizarre figure appeared, this one prancing and gyrating as it appeared around a corner. It was dressed in a white robe with a hood covering its face. Two eye-holes gave it the appearance of a cartoon ghost.

Another inter-title appeared.

THE FOLLOWER!

Victor frowned as the Cursed scuttled around the square, looking in all directions, yet apparently unable to see the Follower as it swaggered and hopped around him, gradually getting closer.

"So the Follower is invisible?"

"Yes," replied Lucy, "an unseen tormentor."

The white-faced young man took out a slip of paper and started to offer it to members of the crowd, all of whom stepped back in exaggerated alarm.

"That's interesting," said Victor. "It implies the curse can be passed on."

The Follower was within arm's length of the Cursed, now, and reached out to snatch the cap off its victim's head. The young man responded with exaggerated alarm, looking around even more frantically. Then the Follower revealed itself by throwing off the white sheet to reveal a second, more elaborate costume underneath; it was a kind of harlequin outfit decorated with odd symbols. The face of the performer was covered in black markings of the same kind.

"Recognize some of those?" asked Lucy, pausing the video for a moment.

Victor nodded.

"Very like those we found in the Book of Hours."

The end of the grotesque pantomime came quickly, now, as the Cursed tried to flee but then stumbled and fell. The Follower struck a triumphant pose over his victim. Then the screen went white and the clip ended.

"And this custom died out when, I wonder?" mused Victor.

"The First World War probably ended it," she said. "A lot of the island's men-folk died, either at sea or in on the Western Front in France. The population of Skara took decades to recover, apparently. There's no evidence of the ritual taking place after 1918, anyway. And all we have before that are a few Victorian references from visitors."

"That's not what ended it. It was the Follower coming back. After that, nobody dared mention it again, let alone put him in a show for bloody tourists."

They looked around, startled, to see Sharkey standing in the office doorway.

***

"Keep going."

That was what the ghost, Billy Straker, had told his old friend. So Mark kept going, hoping that at the end of his journey, there would be some relief from his bizarre ordeal.

Mark arrived in Newcastle, the northernmost city in England, on Friday, where he picked up his rental car. While he didn't like driving on British roads, he had no choice from now on. Skara Farne was twenty miles from the nearest railroad station. He reasoned that at least in the countryside, he would be less likely to get confused by driving on the left side of the road while sitting on the right.

The car had a GPS system, which Brits call a 'Satnav.' The clerk at the rental office explained that the term was short for 'satellite navigation'.

"Yeah," he said, "I got that. I don't think I'll need it where I'm going."

He had heard a lot of stories about how easily GPS got people lost on British roads, or led them into impossible situations and got them stuck. The clerk continued to explain the workings of the Satnav as if Mark hadn't spoken, so he gave up and let the instructions wash over him. When the young man had finished, Mark thanked him and set off into the Friday morning traffic, and promptly got lost in the city's baffling system of one way roads and blind alleys.

Eventually, he pulled over, took out his phone and got the zip code for the Grey Horse, his bed-and-breakfast accommodation. He struggled for a while before he could punch the information into the GPS. It informed him, in a condescending tone, that it was 'calculating the optimum route', then a blue line appeared on the screen and it told him where to go.

"Well, at least it works," he told himself ten minutes later as he left the labyrinthine roads of Newcastle behind and found himself passing through neat suburbs. Soon, he was in the sunlit countryside and started to relax. He realized he had been gripping the wheel, white-knuckled with tension.

"Stay on your current route for fifteen miles," said the robotic voice.

"Yeah, I get it, C3PO," he replied.

"You will reach your destination in approximately one hour," it continued.

"Ever the optimist," he shot back, enjoying the absurdity of bandying words with a microchip.

The device fell silent, there were no other vehicles in sight, and Mark started to take in the landscape. This was obviously sheep country, a place of plenty of rolling hills, sheltered valleys dotted with small villages and farms. A castle came into view, all the more picturesque for being half-ruined. He smiled, remembering when he saw his first English castle. It had amazed him that, to the locals, it was just another old building, of which they had a national surplus.

"Ninety-days were allowed."

For a moment, the words didn't register, then Mark froze,

almost sending the car into a roadside hedge. He managed to hit the brake pedal, then sat for a moment listening to the engine ticking over and the sounds of distant birdsong and bleating sheep.

"What?" he asked, stupidly.

Like it's going to explain itself.

A couple of minutes passed as the sound of a distant aircraft grew and then faded. Mark's heart finally stopped pounding. He looked at the GPS screen, saw nothing but the blue line of his designated route. He heard the sound of another engine and saw a car appear up ahead. He was stopped at an angle in the middle of the narrow road, so he had no choice but to move. As soon as the car started moving, the device spoke up again.

"Follow the road for another fifteen miles."

"Screw you," he replied, but without much force. When he changed gear to tackle an unusually steep hill his hand shook, and he fumbled at the stick, producing a grinding protest from the vehicle.

Did I really hear what I think I heard?

There were only two possible answers, neither of them reassuring. Even with the windows open, the car seemed stuffy under the cloudless June sky. He decided to drive on until he found a place where he could stop and take a break. Luckily, he soon found a small village with a pub, and pulled into the car park. He got out to stretch his legs, and as he closed the car door, a gust of wind blew into his face. He had hoped for a cooling breeze, but was disappointed. If anything, the gust of air was warm.

***

"You're saying he's on his way to Northumberland?" asked Jo.

"I'm afraid so," said Ralph Minns, raising his hands in a gesture of helpless apology. "You haven't been keeping track of his blog?"

Seeing Jo's incomprehension, he led her into his office and clicked on his computer.

"I'm rather proud to have played a small part in young Mark's odyssey," explained Minns. "I worked out his itinerary."

Jo looked at the screen to see a series of blog entries by the American lecturer, evidently recreating a tour of Britain by some long-dead writer. It all seemed innocent enough. It just happened to take Stine far away from her, and any questions she might have had for him.

"So Doctor Stine is going to Skara Farne? That's quite a trek."

"Oh, I agree," said Minns, "but it's all down to the itinerary I prepared for him, you see. It's the trip that Montague Summerskill made just before the First World War, during which he was inspired to write some of his best ghost stories."

The librarian gestured at some dusty boxes on his desk.

"I've been rummaging through the Summerskill papers, they're quite fascinating. A form of detective work, you could say."

"Yes, I'm sure," said Jo, politely. It hadn't taken her long to conclude that Minns was the sort of man who would happily chat all afternoon, to anyone, about anything to do with his job. This might make him an ideal source of information on Morgan, or a total waste of time.

"Of course," Minns went on, "it's all thanks to Dylan Morgan that the papers are in such good order. All neatly filed and cataloged!"

"Morgan? What's he got to do with it?"

"Oh, he did his doctoral thesis on Summerskill back in the Eighties, when he was an undergraduate. And part of his research inevitably involved sorting out the old boy's letters, manuscripts etcetera."

Minns reached into the nearest box and took out a sheaf of papers.

"For instance, these are all Summerskill's letters to his brother, who was a priest in Ireland."

"Fascinating," said Jo. *God, if you exist, please let this not be a coincidence,* she thought.

"Yes," said Minns, "though it's surprising that old Dylan

put young Mark on the Summerskill trail. He's been rather protective of that particular author."

"Protective? You mean secretive, in some way?" she asked.

"Oh, you know how academics are," replied Minns. Then, seeing that she clearly didn't, he went on, "Territorial, I mean. They get an obscure author, write a thesis and then a book or two about them, and this stakes their claim. Sometimes these apparently mild-mannered academics can get very spiteful if someone else offers so much as an opinion on a pet writer. I'm sure detectives don't want other people nosing around on their turf, either, do they?"

"True enough," she conceded. "But let's focus on Morgan. So why do you think he suggested Doctor Stine do research on his territory?"

"Well, he made a point of befriending young Mark when he arrived," mused Minns, evidently thinking about the matter for the first time. "A foreigner in Cambridge often feels like a fish out of water. Especially since some of the older academics regard all newcomers as potential usurpers. The cold shoulder is a common response, I'm afraid."

"But Morgan befriends them," said Jo. "All these potential usurpers?"

"Sometimes, if they're in a similar field," agreed Minns. "Mark Stine, for instance, teaches Gothic fiction, which overlaps with Morgan's area, Victorian and Edwardian literature."

Jo took a deep breath. She had a feeling that her next meeting with Superintendent Masson would be something special, even by his standards.

"You said you'd been working here for over twenty years," she said. "Cast your mind back. Would any of these young lecturers that Morgan befriended have met with sudden, untimely deaths?"

Minns' eyes widened, and he seemed about to laugh. But then he caught himself, and his face took on a more thoughtful expression.

"You know, I do recall an unfortunate accident. In fact, there may have been more than one ..."

***

"You not minding the shop, then?" Sharkey asked. "I could have nicked dozens of them mugs and tee-shirts and bookmarks. Bankrupted your precious Trust."

"What do you mean, about the ritual?" asked Lucy. "What ended it, if not the war?"

Sharkey lumbered into the office, making it suddenly seem far smaller. The fisherman was, thought Victor, somehow too large for the indoor world.

"You shouldn't muck about with that stuff," said Sharkey, nodding at the computer. "But I'm wasting my breath telling you that. So I'll tell you something else. That ritual was a warning, not to tamper with the Abbot's domain. It ended 'cause some fool woke the Follower."

"Who?" asked Lucy.

"Can't recall his name. Some writer from London, or down in the south anyway."

Sharkey gave a dismissive shrug, showing all the true islander's distaste for mainlanders.

"Point is, he woke it, and then the Follower wasn't something you could joke about any more. All that remained of the old customs was a nursery rhyme my mother taught me. Told me to stay away from the Red Abbey, she did, or the Abbot would set his Follower on me."

Victor frowned.

"This is the first I've heard of this."

"It's not something we share with outsiders," declared Sharkey. "You won't find it in your books, or on your computers. But I'll make a gift of it for you now."

He recited.

"Water and earth and fire and air,
Seeks you out and finds you there.

Air and earth and water and fire,
Never does he pause or tire.

Fire and air and water and earth

Rue the day that gave you birth.

Earth and fire and air and water,
Curse is cast, you're lamb to slaughter!"

After a moment's silence, Lucy asked, "Happy childhood, was it?"

Sharkey snorted.

"My old mum knew what she was talking about. Never name it, she told me. Never talk of it, even in whispers, even in roundabout ways. Never mention that other one, either, the one who brought it here, used it against his enemies in olden times. Both bad ones. Never to be mentioned!"

"And yet here you are, positively blabbering on the topic," pointed out Victor.

"No point holding back now, is there?" retorted Sharkey, angrily. "Bloody outsiders, been meddling for years. Over a century. Keep bringing it back, agitating it. And that's bound to end badly. Not just for the victims, either."

He walked over to the office window.

"You're full of dire warnings, Sharkey," she said, "but what can we do about it?"

He stood looking out at the ruins of the Red Abbey.

"Nothing you can do to stop him or his servant."

Victor and Lucy rushed to the window in time to see a robed figure vanish behind one of the few abbey walls still standing.

"Was that him?" asked Lucy. "Abbot Thomas?"

"Oh, aye," said Sharkey. "He never rests easy when the Follower is away. Stir up one, you stir up the other. That's how you can tell the Follower's out tormenting some poor soul. Old Thomas goes on patrol around his old domain."

Chapter 10: The Island

Mark arrived at Skara Farne at high tide. He cursed quietly at his own failure to anticipate a problem that Summerskill had made such a point of emphasizing in his story. The island, the writer had explained, *'is perhaps all the stranger because it is partially linked to the mainland by a causeway that the restless North Sea tides submerge twice a day'.*

The truth of that statement was apparent to Mark as he got out of his hire car and studied the notice board. The next safe crossing time was just under ten minutes from now. Mark could see the causeway already, a tarmac road fringed by dunes emerging from the water. Looking out across the narrow strait, the island looked mysterious, even romantic, with its rugged coastline and distinctive fortress. He could just make out a small village on the landward side, but there was no sign of the Red Abbey. The ruins must be too low-lying and overgrown, he thought.

He was so close to his destination that it was tempting to just drive on. But the sign warned drivers not to attempt to cross simply because they could see that the tide was going out. 'The sea can be treacherous,' it warned. 'WAIT UNTIL THE WAY IS CLEAR'.

If only my way was clear, he thought. *I'm acting on the advice of a dead teenager in the hope that it'll save me from some sort of supernatural tormentor. This is all quite a bump in the road so far as my career plan goes.*

Mark smiled ruefully as he recalled his very ordinary problems of just a few weeks ago. He had been worried about telling Sue he wanted to stay in England. He had been afraid she would break up with him when he broke the news. Now he was in danger of cracking up and in fear of his life. And he still had no idea what he had done, if anything, to deserve such a fate.

Shaking his head at the absurd cruelty of it all, Mark decided to get some air by walking along the beach. He left the road and went off at an angle, down towards the broad beach.

The sky was still almost cloudless, but the June sun seemed lower in the sky here in the north than it had been in Cambridge. That, and a sea breeze, meant he didn't work up much of a sweat as he made his way over grassy dunes onto the wet sand newly exposed by the retreating tide. The sea was azure, dotted with white spots that on closer inspection proved to be seagulls.

So far as Mark could see, he was genuinely alone. For the first time in many days, he didn't feel as if he were being watched. He began to relax, feeling the tension accumulated during the long drive leave his limbs. Remembering childhood holidays, he found a flat stone and tried to skim it. It bounced just the once, plopped into the sea and was gone.

This is a beautiful part of the world, he thought. *And with no-one in sight, I could be in any century. I might see a pirate ship on the horizon, or knights in armor galloping up the coast.*

There was a flurry of motion out at sea, and a gull swept over Mark's head, shrieking plaintively. The cry was taken up by more birds as they took off from the water, protesting loudly, before settling on the dunes behind him. He stared back at the beady eyes peering at him out of the wild grasses, then turned to look out to towards Skara.

At first, Mark could make out nothing that would have bothered the birds. Then he saw a rounded object, maybe thirty yards out. He thought it looked like a swimmer's head, but then Mark realized that he couldn't make out any features. The head was faceless, glistening like jelly. As a short neck and shoulders emerged, it began to register that he was seeing not a person come out of from the water, but the water itself forming a human-like shape.

The Follower. It's real!

Part of him hadn't been sure, unconvinced of the entity's existence despite all the warnings and terrifying events. But now there could be no doubt.

And it was getting closer. Fast.

Heart pounding, Mark turned to run back to the car. The gulls rose again, shrieking as they wheeled over the drama unfolding below them. He glanced back as he scrambled up the first dune and glimpsed at the Follower already on the sand, its huge body shimmering in the sunlight as it strode towards him. Huge, far bigger than any man could be, it moved with a fluid grace. *Literally fluid,* a tiny part of his terrified mind informed him. He had no idea what a giant that was formed out of sea water could do to its victims. All he wanted at that moment was to never find out.

Mark nearly fell going down the third and last dune, then he was back on the road and yanking open the car door. He started the engine and struggled to work the stick-shift with his left hand, hoping to reverse away. Out of the corner of his eye a titanic shape appeared over the dune, grew larger. Mark gave up on reversing, jammed down the accelerator, and sped out onto the causeway. Spray shot out in great arcs and he wondered, way too late, if sea water would cause his hired Nissan to conk out halfway across. The car hit pothole after pothole and Mark fought to keep it on the road.

Mark glanced at the rear view mirror once but saw nothing except white spray and the odd glimpse of blue sky. The windshield was covered in spray as well, reducing visibility to near zero. A looming shape appeared ahead and just to his left, and in an act of instinctive desperation he swerved right. The car lifted onto two wheels, almost rolled over, then fell back. Mark struggled to keep control, failed, and swerved off the road into the dunes. He covered his face with crossed arms just in time as the vehicle came to a jarring halt.

The world seemed to hit him in the face then left him in darkness. When light returned, it was confusing. For a moment, Mark thought of cartoon characters seeing stars after being hit on the head. Then he understood that he was looking at the red and blue flashing lights. The car door opened and a woman leaned inside.

"Driving without a safety belt, breaking the speed limit, and recklessly ignoring a statutory notice. Looks like I got here just in time to book you!"

The face and the voice were familiar but in his stunned condition he took a moment to recall the name.

"Are you that cop who questioned me a while back?"

"Correct," she replied. "And judging from what I just saw

you need all the help you can get. Starting with some first aid."

Mark passed out again.

***

"You're telling me that was Abbot Thomas?" asked Victor.

"Are you telling me it wasn't?" retorted Sharkey. "If you think it's just some fool in fancy dress, maybe you'd better go out and chase him away from your precious ruins?"

Victor didn't move.

"You're saying the abbot's presence proves someone is about to be killed by the Follower? And we can't do anything about it?" demanded Lucy.

"Nobody's ever stopped it before," said Sharkey, turning to leave. "Bad idea to try. Don't get between predator and prey, is my advice. Feel free to ignore an ignorant old man."

As the fisherman left, the phone rang. Victor picked it up.

"Red Abbey?"

He listened for a few moments, and looked at Lucy with surprise.

"Well, yes, I suppose one of us could."

He put the receiver down.

"That was Bill Paterson. Seems he's got a young visitor in his clinic, had a mishap trying to charge across the causeway before low tide."

Lucy gave an irritated shrug.

"So what? There's always some clown who can't read a sign. Or ignores it."

"No," said Victor, looking pensive, "this one was in a flat-spin panic because he was being chased by something inhuman. An entity that's been tormenting him for a while. A police detective brought him in. She's been asking to speak to an expert on the island's folklore."

Lucy was already snatching up her shoulder bag.

"You mind the store, Victor! I'll report back!"

She was already out of the shop before he could say,

"So I told the doc one of us would go down there and offer our expertise."

As the door slammed behind her, Victor looked out at the

ruins again. He couldn't see any one among the tumbled, overgrown stonework. It did not reassure him. He had the distinct sensation of being watched, and wished some tourists would turn up.

***

Mark came around slowly, hearing voices echoing in his head. They were all mixed up, Billy Straker, Brenda, Sue, and some strangers, all talking over each other.

Well done! You got where you needed to be.

Surely that was his mother's voice. But when had she ever congratulated him for anything?

Then the competing voices died, leaving just a conversation between a man and a woman. One he recognized as the police officer who had somehow rescued him on the causeway. The other voice belonged to a man, a stranger with a Scottish accent.

"I know it doesn't make a lot of sense," said Jo Garland, "but I can't ignore the evidence. He's under some kind of paranormal threat. Something way outside the normal realms of police work, at least. I know what I saw when we drove over that hill."

"And what did you see, exactly?"

The Scotsman sounded amused, skeptical.

"I saw something man-shape but much bigger than a man," replied Jo, "moving towards a car that had run off the road. The local officer driving me saw it too. And he saw it vanish, somehow collapse into a pool of sea water among the dunes."

"You're sure you didn't suffer a mild concussion, as well as that young American chap?" asked the doctor.

Mark heard the police officer's voice grow louder in frustration.

"Doctor Paterson, at least four people have been killed by this thing. Probably more. And I don't know how to stop it. If you can't help me do something about it, at least don't leave your patient alone."

"You're serious?" asked Paterson. "I know there's a lot of

local superstition about the Abbot and his supposed powers, but this takes it to a new level."

"It doesn't matter if you believe me," said Jo, "I just need to talk to your folklore expert. Will he be here soon?"

"I'm here now," said a new unfamiliar woman's voice. "Hi! I'm Lucy Hyde."

Mark opened his eyes, saw that he was lying on a bed in a small, neat room. The voices were coming from outside, through an open doorway. He could see no-one and felt a sudden, panicky desire for any kind of human company.

"Hey guys," he said, "can I join in this conversation?"

Doctor Paterson appeared, a young man with a humorous, reassuring manner.

"Mark? Glad you're with us again, you had quite an accident."

The two women followed the doctor into the room. Jo Garland was as he remembered her from their first meeting. She looked serious, professional, but this time she also seemed worried.

She knows how weird this is, he thought. *She's struggling to fit it into her worldview.*

The second woman was tall, with long auburn hair. She looked curiously at Mark.

"So this guy is the victim?" she asked Garland, who nodded in reply.

"Just so we're all on the same page," said Mark, "I've got no problem believing in curses or supernatural beings. And I'd like some help."

Over the next half hour, despite the rational skepticism of Doctor Paterson, they compared notes on the Follower.

***

Sharkey's cottage lay a few hundred yards south of the lighthouse, at the southern end of Monk's Bay. It had become run down in the years since it had ceased to be a family home, but the fisherman made a point of keeping it in some kind of repair. And summer days, like this one, were ideal for fixing the roof.

123

As he worked to secure loose tiles, Sharkey looked out across the bay and wondered. *Would the latest outbreak of evil be the last? It was a century since that over-educated fool had triggered the curse, decades since some other outsider had started using the Follower.*

Nothing lasts forever, he thought.

Then he corrected himself.

Except human folly.

As Sharkey worked, he gradually became aware of a presence nearby. He didn't turn to look, but at one point his hand slipped as he was fixing a tile and he bruised his hand.

"Have you got nowhere better to go, you old bugger?" he cried in anger.

He looked behind him, but there was nobody there. He turned to resume work, but then a gust of wind struck him. A sturdy man, he was in no danger of being dislodged. But he knew better than to stay in the open and began to scramble down from the roof. As he did so, he looked around he saw a depression appear in the grass a few yards away. It moved rapidly around the cottage in a spiral, the wild vegetation being pushed down by an invisible force.

It's on the island, then, he thought. *But it's still on the hunt! Whoever it wants must be here!*

This had never happened in Sharkey's lifetime. This was something new.

***

"That's it?" said Jo. "That slip of paper with some doodling on it?"

After all she had seen, and all the death and misery Morgan had left in his wake, the slip of rice-paper seemed utterly trivial. Yet Miranda Bell had been clear enough. Paper. Symbols. Concealed in a book. It was obvious Morgan's method hadn't changed over the years, like many a serial killer before him.

"This is what I found in the spine of the book he gave me," confirmed Mark.

"Can I see?" Lucy reached out, but Mark jerked the paper

back.

"I don't think that's a good idea," he explained. "If you accept it you become the target."

Paterson snorted in contempt.

"For god's sake, man, this is the twenty-first century!"

Mark held out the paper to him.

"Would you care to examine it more closely?"

Paterson hesitated, then said to Jo, "Look, I'm not feeding into this collective madness. Don't overtire the patient. That's a basic principle you might consider, people."

He left, slamming the door.

"Poor Bill, he really never got the whole island vibe," remarked Lucy, sitting down by the bed.

Mark put the paper back in his wallet.

"What I don't get is why?" he said to Jo. "Why me?"

"Resentment," she said simply. "You're a young interloper in his academic field. On his turf. He may have done away with a couple of other potential usurpers. You see the same thing with drug gangs. It's just they use bullets, not ..."

She nodded at the slip of rice-paper.

Lucy Hyde frowned.

"But how did he acquire this ability in the first place?"

Jo shrugged, uninterested in theoretical matters. But Mark had an answer.

"Montague Summerskill. A writer who came here just over a hundred years ago, and did some research into Abbot Thomas and his occult powers. The Follower killed him."

"Someone cursed him, this writer?" asked Lucy.

"No," said Mark. "I just figured that out. He cursed himself. And unwittingly gave Morgan a convenient murder method."

Seeing the women's puzzlement, Mark asked for the paperback of ghost stories. Lucy got it from the locker where Mark's possessions had been stored. He flipped through to the back of the Gadabout edition of The Dark Isle, then handed it to her.

"You see? At the back, there's an unfinished story, written in the form of a letter."

"How does that help?" asked Jo.

"It's not a story at all," explained Mark. "All Summerskill's papers were kept together at St Caedmon's library. Morgan, as a student, was probably the first person to read them all since Summerskill died. And he classified them into fiction, scholarship, personal letters and so on."

Lucy was skimming the so-called unfinished story.

"So this is not fiction, but fact? Listen to this! *I recklessly invoked an ancient evil using certain arcane symbols and a simple incantation. It was a moment of foolishness, my dear brother, for which I fear I must pay heavily.*'"

Lucy looked up, eyes wide.

"He didn't realize what he was doing, that it was real! He had spent so long writing ghost stories that it never occurred to him that supernatural evil could be real!"

Jo frowned in puzzlement.

"But if he knew he was cursed why didn't he pass the paper to someone else?"

"Who?" asked Mark. "Who would he pass it to? Bearing in mind he was an old-school gentleman. The idea of passing it on probably never crossed his mind. He was a good man."

"There must be a way to neutralize the curse," said Lucy, half to herself. "Perhaps destroying the paper?"

"I think Katrina Lawless burned the slip that Morgan gave her," pointed out Jo. "That didn't achieve anything. So she and her friend probably did some research, concocted their own curse, and then slipped the paper to Morgan in his own copy of that book. They were a lot cleverer than he thought."

Jo nodded to Mark.

"It was inevitable that Morgan would pass it on to someone once he realized he was in trouble. He might have done it to anyone, he's probably a psychopath, but you were the ideal target, I suppose."

"That means there were two curses in play at the same time," pointed out Lucy. "But only one Follower? How bizarre. I'm surprised that didn't gum up the works, somehow."

Jo shrugged. She was out of her depth with all this occult speculation, and starting to feel despair. She had a clear duty to protect a member of the public from violence. She was surprised to find that the oath she had taken on becoming an officer still meant so much to her. At the time it had seemed like a minor ritual, but now it loomed large in her mind. Jo would never forget Miranda Bell's mother, the terrible sound of her pain and despair. A woman scrabbling at the wreckage of her home to get to her daughter's corpse.

If this man dies, it's on me.

The simple thought crystallized an idea that had been forming in her mind for a while.

"Give it to me," she said to Mark. "Give it to me, I'll take it back to Cambridge, and confront Morgan with it. Demand that he take the curse off. You two stay here and try to find another solution, some way to help before ..."

Jo didn't finish the sentence, but instead held out her hand.

"I hereby take that piece of paper voluntarily, and will face the Follower if I have to. It's my duty."

They objected, of course, which was heartening in a way. But it also underlined how serious the threat was.

"Hand it over," said Jo bluntly. "Or you'll die. You'll die a stupid, painful, early death like Juliet and Katrina, or you'll live on as a vegetable for a few years like Miranda Bell. Hand it over, Stine."

God, Jo thought, *do I have to punch a sick man and take it by force?*

"Mister Stine," she said, leaning over the bed, "under English law, it is a criminal offense to withhold evidence from a police officer in the course of her investigations. Give it here!"

Reluctantly, like a man handling some poisonous creature, Mark held out the slip of paper. She took it between finger and thumb. It was almost weightless. And yet, at that moment, Jo could have sworn that a great burden fell upon her shoulders. And she had a sudden sense that there were more than three people in the small clinic room.

"Right, I'd better get going. But before I set off, what can I expect?"

Mark told her as much as he could.

"Ghosts," Jo said. "I reckon I can handle them. And the only thing that really scares me is letting people down."

Chapter 11: Countdown

When he handed over the slip, Mark felt as if a veil had been torn from his eyes. Suddenly everything in the room seemed brighter, the colors clearer. It was only then that he realized what a shadowy, bleak world he had inhabited for the last few weeks.

I'm free, he thought. *Free of the fear. But only because somebody else has been damn braver and smarter.*

"It would help if I knew how long I've got," said Jo Garland as she folded the paper and put it inside her jacket. "Not much point in going back to Cambridge if I get killed halfway down the road."

"All we know is that ninety-nine days were allowed," said Lucy. "But that's no help if we don't know when the students cast their curse."

"Your phone," said Mark to Jo. "Try your phone."

"Won't work on the island," put in Lucy.

"That's not what I mean," he replied. "I tried to make appointments on the calendar app on my phone. And on my laptop. What if nothing like that works beyond the crucial date? Maybe it's part of the curse, deleting you from the future?"

"That's quite a stretch, but right now I'll take it," said Jo, taking out her phone. She worked at it for a few moments, then frowned.

"July is out, so it's this month."

After another five seconds of experimentation, she looked up.

"I can't get the damn thing to work after Thursday. Looks like I'd better get a move on."

Today's Tuesday, thought Mark. *How the hell can we come up with anything in time to save her?*

Before Mark or Lucy could think of anything to say, the detective was leaving with a cheerful, "Nice meeting you. See you again soon."

Mark doubted that very much, and hoped his lack of confidence didn't show.

"Is there any way to stop this?" he asked Lucy. "Anything you know of?"

She shrugged in despair.

"Everything we know suggests the curse must run its course. The Follower can't be turned aside or blocked."

"Then we need to look harder, think harder!" he shouted, then fell back onto the pillow a jolt of pain shot through his head and neck.

"Are you okay?" said Lucy, getting up and putting a palm on his forehead. "You're a bit feverish. Bill Paterson said you'd need an X-ray when you get back to the mainland, maybe even a brain scan."

He laughed, which produced another, milder spasm of pain.

"We live in a world of space-age hardware, but we can't stop a medieval curse."

"We've only just figured out what we're up against," she pointed out. "Maybe we can still beat it. Anything's possible."

***

Dylan Morgan poured himself a large Scotch and raised the glass in a toast to his cat, Cassandra. The animal looked on, incurious. She had seen him get drunk far too often to find the process interesting.

"You think this might be a premature celebration, eh, old girl?" he asked. "Rhetorical question, no need to answer! Point is, Cass, I've won again. Every time they try to thwart me, belittle me, push me aside, I beat 'em. Here's to a well-earned victory!"

Morgan gulped a mouthful of the single malt whiskey.

"That hits the spot," he said. "Very palatable."

Cassandra yawned, jumped off the small table, and stalked out of the main cabin, through the galley, and into the tiny sleeping berth at the bows of the boat.

"Ah, the eternal feminine, ever in need of her beauty sleep!" mused Morgan.

He went up onto the deck of his boat, glass in hand, and surveyed the riverside district of Cambridge.

My domain, he thought. *My realm. I fell in love with this place as a freshman and swore I'd make it my own, or at least my own little corner of it. And I did! By a ridiculous fluke, I found a way to prevail against the petty, the stupid, and the vengeful. All my enemies, destroyed!*

An attractive young woman was going by, pushing a double buggy containing cute, dark-eyed twin girls. A man walked alongside, trying to keep a small dog on a long leash from zooming off in random directions. Morgan nodded to the family, called 'Good morning!' The man returned the greeting, the woman smiled rather thinly. They didn't want to stop and chat.

You see a drunken old fool, boozing on a weekday morning, he thought, smiling benignly. *Someone to ignore or make fun of, I suppose? Oh, I could happily show you terror and death for your impertinence.*

"Mister Morgan?"

He turned to see the young policewoman. *What was her name, Gartree? Garland?* He forgot names so easily nowadays. Remembering their last encounter, he put on an expression of injured innocence.

"Sergeant? This really does start to feel like police harassment. I am quite serious when I say I will make a formal complaint."

"Oh, don't be like that," she replied, stepping onto the small aft deck of the boat. "This is strictly an informal call."

Morgan noticed that the woman was dressed much less formally than last time. In fact, her short skirt, heels, and tight blouse were more play than work. Especially, he noted, since the top two buttons of her blouse were undone.

"Informal, you say?" he asked, tentatively.

"I just wanted to apologize for our misunderstanding the other day," said Jo, smiling and gazing into his eyes. "I was rather upset about Miranda Bell's death and I'm afraid it affected my judgment."

Morgan smiled back, relaxing. He was on familiar ground again.

They can't resist me, he thought. *Deep down, they're all the same. It's the combination of power, intellect, and raw animal appeal that does it.*

"Ah, that's quite all right my dear," he said, "I know how stressful life can be, especially for young ladies like yourself."

He held up the glass.

"I was just having a little drink. Would you care to join me? Or are you on duty, Sergeant Garland?"

She looked coy, but then gave another smile.

She really is quite pretty when she takes the trouble, Morgan thought. *Most feminine. Nothing special, of course, but I wouldn't say no.*

"Well, it's my day off," she replied, "so perhaps a small one wouldn't hurt? And please, call me Jo!"

"Jo it is!" he exclaimed, leading the way into the cabin. "And call me Dylan. I hope you like whiskey, Jo, it's all I've got at this moment. Or any other moment, to be honest."

"That's fine," she replied, looking around. "Could I clear a few of these books off a seat, Dylan?"

"By all means, my dear," he said as he went to look for another glass. "Clear away the intellectual detritus of yesteryear, let us live for the moment!"

"I'll certainly drink to that!" she said, putting her small sequined purse on the window sill.

***

Detective Superintendent Masson had spent a lively few hours in a meeting with his superiors. It had not gone well, as he had been unable to explain why his personal protégée had gone absent without leave. He returned to his own department convinced he was well on the way to a coronary.

"I don't suppose there's any news of her, Lewis?" he barked at a senior detective.

"No sir, she's not picking up, and the uniforms we sent to her flat got no reply."

"But she's not on that bloody island anymore, that Skara place?" demanded Masson.

"No sir, she was there for a few hours, according to the local police. They were a bit suspicious of her story, but they thought she had your authority to operate outside our area."

Where the hell is she, thought Masson, *and what's she playing at? Does she want to go back to traffic duty? Or end up as a security guard for some crappy private outfit?*

"There is one odd thing, though," said Lewis.

Masson gave him a baleful glare.

"Another one? Oh, great. All right, what?"

"Before she left, Garland seems to have done some research on old civil defense sites in this area," explained Lewis. "She accessed files on the central government database."

"Civil defense?" Masson was baffled, a sensation he was getting used to. "What would she want that for?"

Lewis shrugged.

"Only thing I can think of is that she wanted some kind of a bolt-hole. Somewhere to hide."

"Hide from what, for Christ's sake?" yelled Masson, finally losing his temper. Heads turned across the open-plan office. "And don't say from me, Lewis, if you know what's good for you."

"No, sir. What's our next move, sir?"

Masson took a breath, calmed down, and considered.

"All we can do is keep looking, keep calling her phone. And if that doesn't work, this afternoon, take a couple of uniforms round the nearest sites she checked out, just in case."

"Shall I put out an all-points bulletin on her car, sir?" asked Lewis, in carefully neutral tone.

"No, I'm not going that far yet," said Masson. "I'm not treating one of our own as a criminal. Not yet."

Not for at least another day, he thought, as he went into his office and closed the door. *If I can just keep the top brass at bay a bit longer. She deserves that much.*

His phone began to ring.

***

Jo had wondered if she had overdone her make-up and clothes. Maybe she had put on too much of one and too little of the other to be credible. But Morgan seemed to be lapping it up. She also wondered how the old lecher could mistake the fixed grin on her face for a seductive smile. But, she reflected, he wasn't the first man to see what he wants to see.

"Now, I hope you're not trying to get me tipsy!" she said, as she took a glass of Scotch from his pudgy hand. He leaned over her, very close in the cramped cabin, and peered brazenly down her cleavage.

"As if I would!" he said, taking a seat on the opposite side of the cabin.

They were close, but not quite close enough to touch. She had hoped he would sit next to her and begin pawing at her straight away. He certainly seemed the type. But now it seemed there would have to be a flirtation of sorts.

"Yes, Dylan," she said. "I really had to come and say sorry for the rude way I treated you before. It was most unprofessional."

She took a sip of Scotch and tried not to gag.

Older men keep giving me strong drinks, she thought. *I really should think about my life choices, but it's a bit late now.*

"My dear, I quite understand," said Morgan, waving away the issue. "You were upset by witnessing a terrible accident. That poor girl. And her mother, too. An appalling tragedy."

Jo put on what she hoped was a pout.

"Yes, but that was no excuse for jumping to silly conclusions about an innocent person like yourself, Dylan. As if you could cast spells on people."

She attempted a giggle.

"It's just silly, isn't it?"

He looked slightly peeved by that remark.

"Well, not so silly to our ancestors, who believed in the power of curses and so on."

"Yes," she countered, "but in this day and age, who would believe it? I was just being silly."

She gave another giggle, hoping she sounded less than sober, and at the same time crossed her legs for good measure. She could tell from his expression that it had had the desired effect.

"Anyway," she went on, "I'm sure all those girls were just being spiteful. I see a lot of that, foolish young girls getting obsessed with mature men, imagining they're part of some great romance, then going to pieces and turning into total psychos. It's very sad, really."

"Oh, let's not be too unkind," said Dylan, clearly enjoying the turn the conversation had taken. "Speaking ill of the dead, and all that."

She leaned forward, trying to judge the angle so he got the best possible view.

"You should try a girl who's had a bit more experience," she murmured. "A few more miles on the clock, so to speak."

**

"This is it?" asked Mark.

The altar stone looked like nothing but a bit of old rubble. It took a more skilled eye, he concluded, to see it as a precious historical artifact. But it was more than that, it was the lair of an inhuman killer of an almost unimaginable kind.

"Get up really close," urged Lucy, crouching by the altar. "You can just make out the markings."

Mark followed her advice, and recognized a couple of the symbols from the slip of rice-paper.

"And these are symbols for the ancient elements? Earth, air, fire and water?"

"That's where the evidence points," she replied. "The four elements, or the four humors when they were applied to the human body."

Victor Carew walked around the altar, filming with his phone. Then he showed Mark the result.

"See? Or rather, do you not see?"

Mark looked from the screen to the stone and back. It was true. The images didn't show up on camera.

"We think it means the Follower is out on a mission, so to speak," said Victor. "And that the carvings will show up when it returns."

"We have old archive photos that definitely show the carvings," added Lucy. "Presumably during the long years when it was inactive."

"Yes, but what is it?" Mark demanded. "All this research,

speculation, where does it get us? Or more to the point, how does it help Jo Garland?"

"We're as frustrated as you are," pointed out Victor. "But if we can't beat this thing with knowledge, what else is there?"

Mark looked down at the carvings again.

"The four elements," he said. "So it can make itself a temporary body, in a sense, out of air, fire, water, or earth. It drowned Summerskill, burned two of my students, smashed Miranda's home with a localized windstorm."

"Hard to defend against that kind of power," said Victor. "I mean, you can steer clear of water, but the rest?"

"She's smart," said Lucy. "I could tell that she had given this a lot of thought. Maybe she can come up with something nobody else has thought of."

Mark stood up, looked out over the strait towards the mainland.

"God, I hope so."

***

Morgan could hardly believe his luck. The detective he had classed as a typical strait-laced bitch, one of the myriad inferiors dedicated to putting him down, had turned out to be quite the little tart. Gone was the hard-faced career woman, she was all boobs, legs, and mascara! It was almost a miracle. Of course, she had a few more miles on the clock than he preferred, but he was no spring chicken. And there would be something deliciously satisfying in taking carnal pleasure from a woman who had challenged him, and failed. Another glorious victory!

When Jo got up and wobbled over on her heels to sit beside him, he had a moment's doubt.

Is this too good to be true?

But what harm could it possibly do? Here she was, drinking his whiskey, laughing at his jokes, and best of all wriggling her neat posterior on the same bench. He could smell her perfume, feel her warmth as her thigh pressed against his.

Face it, Dylan old boy, you've still got what it takes! They simply can't resist you.

He began to run his hands over her, and she went through the motions of fending him off, giggling to make it clear it was all just a formality.

Thank God I didn't start on the booze a few hours earlier, he thought. *Wouldn't want to disappoint the poor girl!*

"I really shouldn't be doing this!" she breathed in his ear. "It's very wrong for an officer to have any kind of liaison with a person involved in a case."

"Really?" he said. "Well, that makes you a very naughty young lady indeed, doesn't it?"

"Oh yes," she said, "it will just have to remain our little secret!"

He had unbuttoned her blouse when Cassandra walked into the cabin. The cat sat down on the threshold peering at the humans.

"I forgot about your nice pussycat!" said Jo. "Surely, she's not going to watch?"

"Oh, ignore Cass," Morgan replied, nuzzling at her, "she's seen far more outrageous things, believe me!"

Suddenly the cat spat, started to retreat back into the galley. Morgan and Jo both paused for a moment as Cassandra's fur stood on end. The animal backed a few more paces then turned and vanished into the foremost cabin in a blur of orange.

"I don't think she likes sharing you with me," said Jo, running her fingers through his hair. "What a jealous pussy!"

"Yes," said Morgan, flatly. A great leaden weight seemed to have formed in the pit of his stomach. Suddenly he was stone-cold sober. He got to his feet, shoving the woman aside, and looked down at her.

My god, she was going to trick me! It was all just an act!

"You've got it! He gave it to you!" he shouted.

His heart raced in panic.

Oh my god, it must be close, very close, he thought. *There can't be more than a few hours, at most.*

"What are you talking about, Dylan?" she asked, feigning innocence. "What have I done?"

For a moment, he doubted himself, she looked so wide-eyed and innocent, but then his anger flared up again.

"Cassandra was fine with you before! She reacted like that when those little bitches laid the curse on me! You treacherous whore!"

He raised a clenched fist, almost blinded by rage and fear.

"How could you do this to me?" he shouted. "You conniving slut, I'll kill you myself!"

But before he could hit her, she had grabbed his other arm and spun him around. Off balance, he fell forward and hit his face against the aft bulkhead. He tried to struggle but she was frighteningly strong and very fast. Somehow she had both his hands, and he felt cold metal against his wrists.

There was a sharp click, and he realized she had handcuffed him.

"That was unlucky, Dylan," she said, kneeling in the small of his back. "Thirty seconds more and you'd have taken it off me, of your own free will."

"What the hell are you talking about? Of course I wouldn't!" he bellowed.

"Oh, you would have," she said. "I ruined two perfectly good brassieres 'till I found one I could fit that bloody paper inside."

From his awkward position on his knees with his face shoved into the threadbare carpet, he saw her step over him and retrieve her purse. As she opened it she asked, almost casually, if he had any known heart problems.

"What?" he shouted. "Let me go!"

"You really should tell me," she said, kneeling down next to him. She showed him a small, black plastic box. When she pressed a button on the side, a spark jumped across electrical contacts at one end.

"Now," she repeated. "Do you have any heart problems? Because even if you don't, it's not a good idea to make me use this. So best come quietly, Dylan. We're going on a little adventure."

Chapter 12: The Follower

Once she had gotten the cuffs on him, Morgan was subdued, at least at first. Jo had found that that was usually the way of it. They either went crazy and screamed to high heaven from the start or went along with you. But, after she had bundled him into the back seat of her car, Morgan recovered his composure enough to start protesting. He kept it up, loud and long, as she drove them out of Cambridge.

"This is wrongful arrest! You're committing a crime, illegally detaining me!"

She ignored him until he came up with the inevitable one, put in a more placatory tone.

"Look, just let me go now and we'll say no more about it, eh?"

Jo felt cold anger possess her.

"We'll say no more about Katrina, and Juliet? We'll say no more about Miranda Bell, or Sylvia Bayo, or any of the others?"

That silenced Morgan, but she pressed on, needing to vent.

"We'll say no more about you being a serial murderer, and just let you get on with it? And the next time some hapless student or ambitious colleague upsets you, we'll say nothing when they die, too?"

She looked up at the rear view mirror, saw his ashen face, his frightened eyes.

The closer he is to me, the more danger he's in. He knows it.

"No, Dylan, that's not how it goes. We're going to have a long talk about this, and as the clock ticks down maybe you'll even tell me how to stop it."

She saw his mind working, calculating, his alcohol-sodden brain coming up with possible ploys.

"Yes!" he said, "Of course I will. I'll tell you exactly how to take the curse off, if you promise to let me go. That's fair, isn't it?"

Jo felt her heart sink, then. She knew now how this one

would have to play out.

"Yeah," she replied. "Because I can trust you not to tell me some bullshit bit of abracadabra that wouldn't work? You've got no idea how to stop it, have you Dylan?"

"Just let me go you bloody bitch!" he screamed, kicking the back of her seat in baffled rage. He kept it up for a good half mile.

"I don't want to have to waste time, old man," she said, when he paused to gasp for air, "but if I have to stop and taser your flabby arse, I will."

That silenced him for a good ten minutes, by which time they had reached the bunker.

***

Mark looked at the video of the folk ritual. He flinched when the follower threw back its absurd sheet to reveal the bizarre figure decorated with symbols. He stopped the video and wound back to the moment when the Abbot appeared, but found no clue there.

"Victor and I have watched it dozens of times," said Lucy. "It doesn't seem to offer any hope."

"There must be something," said Mark.

Lucy looked at him for a moment, then said, "Well, there's you and the journey you've made."

"What do you mean?" he asked.

"Why did you end up here, of all places? The place where Summerskill first unearthed the secret of Abbot Thomas, and the Follower?"

Mark pondered the question.

"When I was knocked out earlier I heard someone telling me I was in the right place. Something like that. It's hazy."

"And from what you've said about the ghost you saw," said Lucy, "the curse might not be working in the way it normally does. It usually drives people almost insane with fear, after all. Yet you say you met an old friend who gave you advice?"

"True," he conceded. "But maybe that's because it wasn't meant for me? Perhaps passing it on changes the effect, somehow?"

Lucy grimaced in frustration, gazed at the laptop screen with its frozen image of a long-dead ritual.

"So much we don't know, and so little time!"

Mark spoke without thinking, then.

"It's a pity we can't just ask Abbot Thomas."

Lucy looked at him, mouth open.

"My god, that's it! You're a genius, Mark! Why not simply ask him?"

Before he could say anything else, she had rushed out of the room, saying she had to fetch something from what sounded like 'the lighthouse'.

***

After changing into a pair of runners, Jo had hauled Morgan out the car. Subduing him again with the threat of the taser, she dragged him towards the gates of the complex. Red warning notices informed trespassers that they would be prosecuted. That was the least of her worries.

More concerning was the possibility that the security cameras she could see around the perimeter were working and that someone was at the other end watching for intruders in real time. From what she knew it was unlikely, but there was still a risk she would be interrupted before their time was up. The last thing she needed was to endanger innocent bystanders.

"We won't be disturbed here. I called in some favors to get access. A trick I learned from my boss," Jo explained. "You'd probably get along with him, he likes a drink."

Morgan had taken to moaning, with the odd word or two being audible. Jo heard threats, pleas, and abuse in about equal measure.

"Looks like some old friends waiting for you," she remarked, trying to sound confident.

The ghosts were standing inside the padlocked gates. Jo recognized Miranda Bell, pale and dark-eyed, and the two students, Katrina and Juliet. A tall Nigerian woman was presumably Sylvia Bayo, and there were others, six or seven, standing further back. Mostly young women, but there were a couple of young men, too.

For a moment, she felt daunted, afraid to trespass further in a realm she knew nothing about. But her captive's cowardly reaction restored her confidence.

"No!" shouted Morgan. "If they're here then it must be close!"

As she unlocked the gates, Jo found herself thinking aloud.

"Interesting, isn't it? They're your ghosts, apart from Miranda. I was there when she died. But the rest, they're your victims. Yet the curse is still on me."

She let the padlock fall, undid the chain, and pushed one creaking gate open a couple of feet. She shoved Morgan through, hoping he didn't think to simply curl up on the ground. No way could she carry him, and the taser wouldn't really help get him moving.

"Because," she went on, "I reckon you've overdone it, Dylan. I think you've abused this power, whatever it is. Maybe broken some law. Not a man-made law, no, we can't get you on any of those. But there are others, I'm sure. And I think you might have pissed off whoever's in charge of enforcing them."

He looked at her and she could see her words had struck home.

"What do you know?" he spluttered, trying to look defiant. "I've researched this subject for decades!"

"Yes," she retorted, pushing him towards a square, weather-beaten structure that squatted amid luxuriant weeds. "And what have you done with your great knowledge? Killed some people. Whoop-de-do, aren't you the criminal mastermind."

"What is this place?" he demanded.

She paused in unlocking the steel door set into the concrete blockhouse. She tried not to look at the ghosts crowding around them.

"Somewhere secure, I hope. At least it's worth a try."

"You can't stop it with walls and doors!" he shouted.

She dragged open the door, revealing steel four inches thick.

"Maybe not old-school fortifications," she said, pushing

him ahead of her into the darkness. "But let's see what Cold War technology can do."

***

"If Bill Paterson catches us doing this, we'll be barred from his practice," commented Victor.

He and Lucy were seated to one side of Mark's bed. The small wheeled table used for Mark's meals now bore a Ouija board.

"Oh, Bill will be down the pub for the rest of the afternoon," said Lucy. "Probably not be back till late, as its darts night."

Mark looked at the lacquered wooden board with its ring of letters, plus two words, Yes and No. It looked ancient, an antique from a bygone age of cranks and charlatans. He would have laughed at the idea of using one even as a party game just a few weeks ago. Now he felt a deep, irrational hope that it might reveal a way to thwart the Follower at the last minute.

"You really think Abbot Thomas will just answer questions? Through this thing?"

"It's worth a try," said Lucy. "Admittedly, I've not had much luck with this before, but I get a feeling you're more sensitive to such things."

"Really?" he said, oddly flattered.

"Can we just get on?" said Victor, taking a water glass from the tray atop Mark's locker and putting it upside down in the center of the board.

Each placed a finger on top of the glass.

Lucy took a deep breath, exhaled, and then asked, "Is any spirit here that wishes to communicate?"

Nothing happened for a few seconds, then the glass started to slide slowly towards the Yes.

"Could be unconscious bias, involuntary muscle movements," muttered Victor, only to be shushed by Lucy.

"Is the spirit of Abbot Thomas here?" she asked.

This time there was no movement.

"Perhaps he doesn't understand modern English?" suggested Victor.

142

Lucy shot him an annoyed glance.

Before they could begin arguing, Mark asked, "Is the spirit of Montague Summerskill here?"

This time the glass jerked back and forth, jabbing at the word Yes.

"The man on the bicycle!" said Lucy.

"Do you have a message for anyone here?" asked Mark.

More jabbing, an emphatic Yes.

"Can you give us your message now?" asked Lucy, eagerly.

The glass began to glide back and forth, fast and with precision.

A message began to appear.

***

The ghosts followed them down into the tunnels, and as they left the noise of the surface world behind, Jo became aware of the phantoms' whispering voices. They were all asking questions of Morgan, demanding to know why, what had they done to deserve their monstrous fate. He didn't reply, at least not at first, but after a while, he started to shout at them to shut up, leave him alone.

Morgan's voice echoed in the concrete tunnels. His victims' voices didn't.

"Shut it, Dylan, we've arrived," said Jo, pushing him into the deepest chamber.

"What is this place? Why have you brought me here?"

Jo pushed the heavy steel door shut behind them and locked it. Like the tunnels, the survival room was lit by low-powered emergency lights. It was bare except for bunks on one wall, plus a couple of metal chairs. She sat Dylan in one, pulled the other opposite his so she could face him.

"Two reasons. One is that a few thousand tons of steel and concrete above and around us might keep your nasty little friend out. After all, it was designed to stop a nuclear blast from killing the VIPs in here."

She held up the taser to silence his renewed protests.

"Oh, I know, it's a long shot. But worth a try. The other reason is simple. We're well away from anyone else who might get hurt. You know, the way Juliet Archer got burned to death because you put a curse on her friend?"

"There's still time!" he rasped. He had almost lost his voice from shouting. "Just let me go and I'll save you!"

She recoiled from his drink-laden breath.

"Sorry, Dylan, but I think you're just turning on the charm to get what you want."

Jo stood up and went to sit on one of the bunks while Morgan descended into shrieking incoherent abuse at her, his victims, and life in general.

"I wouldn't use up too much air, Dylan," she said. "The emergency lights work but the air-con doesn't. Closed-cycle system, you see. No link to the surface so no fallout could get sucked in. We can only breathe what was in here when I shut that door."

That silenced him, but then he began to plead with her again, alternating promises with ever more violent threats. His voice gave out completely soon after. Then they sat in the half-light while the ghosts thronged around Morgan, whispering their endless reproaches.

***

"A couple of people saw an officer shoving a man who answers to Morgan's description into a vehicle that could be hers," said Lewis, handing Masson a printout. "When someone asked what was going on, she flashed a police ID at them. The witness was skeptical because of the way she was dressed."

Masson raised an eyebrow as he read the report.

Dressed for a party? She must have tried some kind of honey-trap, he thought.

"But no news from any of those civil defense sites?" asked Masson.

"Uniforms taking their time, sir," replied Lewis. "It's not easy to check them, what with their being mostly underground complexes."

Underground, thought Masson. *Suppose she's hiding from a being that somehow knocks down regular buildings. Like a bomb-blast.*

"Okay, Lewis," he said, "get on that computer and find me the deepest bunker in the county. I'll get a car sorted, and we'll go straight there."

Masson was turning away, then he paused and added, "Oh, and get a couple of really powerful torches, the waterproof variety."

"We're going underground, boss?" asked Lewis.

"Looks like it, son," replied Masson. "Let's just hope we come back up again. Oh, and there's some special equipment I want you to bring."

***

At first, Jo thought the oxygen was starting to run out. The concrete chamber, which had been cold, began to feel warmer. Then the ghost vanished. One moment, the wraiths of Morgan's victims were standing around him, like a Greek chorus of reproach. Then they were gone.

Jo stood up and walked around Morgan, who was slumped sideways, eyes half-shut. A layer of spittle dribbled from the corner of his mouth.

In other circumstances, I might have pitied you, old man, she thought. *But not now. Not after what I've seen, what I know.*

"I see your friends and lovers have deserted you, Dylan," she said.

He jerked upright, looked around the room.

"It's close by!" he croaked. "The torment is nearly over!"

Jo realized that as she crossed the room, the heat increased, and she turned to face the door. The metal wasn't glowing, but when she reached out her arms towards it the palms of her hands felt unpleasantly warm.

It must be trying to melt its way through, she thought. *Let's hope whoever made that blast door did a proper job.* As the heat level rose, Jo retreated to a far corner, leaving Morgan to sweat nearer to the door. After a while, the temperature began to fall, and Jo wondered if that was it. Perhaps she had beaten the Follower, whatever it was?

Everything has its limits, she told herself. *Sooner or later, even the most powerful killer meets his, or its, match.*

She jumped as the door rang with a tremendous impact, as if a sledgehammer had struck it. Morgan, too, had been shocked, so much that he fell off his chair and sprawled on the concrete. Another impact came, deafening in the enclosed space, and Jo thought she saw the door jump on its hinges.

Or was that me reacting? Hard to tell.

Jo could hear the windstorm outside, now, as it roared up and down the tunnels in seeming frustration before hurling itself against the metal again. Morgan was half-crawling, half-wriggling away towards the other far corner, maximizing the distance between Jo and the Follower. She got up and went over to him, knelt down on the cold floor.

"No, Dylan, we're in this together," she said, between deafening metallic booms. "If you can't save me, you can't save yourself."

His only reply was a whimper as he curled up in the corner, facing the wall.

As suddenly as they had started, the deafening blows ended and Jo heard the weird subterranean wind die down.

"Round two to me, I think," she remarked. "That's fire and air found wanting. Water isn't likely, as there's no supply of any kind in here. Cut off long ago."

That only leaves earth, she thought. *Sylvia Bayo died out jogging one morning because the earth seemed to simply swallow her up.*

She tried to remember the details of the plans she had studied all too briefly.

They protected this place from blast damage and firestorms happening above ground, she thought. *But how thick did they think the floor needed to be?*

***

"That's her car," said Lewis as they screeched to a stop outside the old civil defense complex. "And the gates are open."

The officers ran into the compound and, after a moment's hesitation, Lewis pointed out the entrance to the deep bunker network.

"Right," said Masson, "I'll go in first, you follow. And don't drop that, whatever you do."

He nodded at the First Aid kit Lewis carried.

"Right behind you, boss!"

Once inside, they were faced with two tunnels, and Lewis began to fumble with the blueprints showing the layout of the complex.

"Make it quick!" rasped Masson, holding up his flashlight. The emergency lights were too weak to read by.

But before they could study the plan, they heard a distant roar.

Is that an underground train? thought Masson. *No, it can't be. So what the hell is it?*

Then he remembered the security camera footage from the Bell case.

"Get down!" he shouted, throwing himself flat on the floor.

Lewis followed orders instinctively, flattening himself on the rough, dirty concrete. They were just in time. A tremendous blast of warm air erupted from the left-hand corridor, and Masson found himself clawing at the floor of the tunnel to stop himself from being dragged out of the main door.

As suddenly as it had appeared, the unnatural hurricane had gone.

"Shit! I lost the chart," exclaimed Lewis, as they scrambled to their feet.

"I think we know which corridor to take," said Masson, shining his flashlight on torn papers and other debris lying around them. "That thing will have left quite a trail. We have to follow it."

"What was that, sir?" asked Lewis, trying to keep his voice steady.

"No idea, son," replied Masson, "but there's a good chance it'll be back. Let's get moving!"

***

There was a rumbling noise, like a distant train heard approaching an underground platform. The walls shook, and Jo saw the stained concrete under her feet blossom with hairline cracks. Morgan began to whimper more loudly.

"Looks like the final round, Dylan," she said, sitting with her back to the wall, taser held out in front of her. It seemed an absurdly feeble weapon.

Never confront a dangerous individual without proper backup. She smiled at what Masson would say about her breaking that basic rule. *Not to mention about a dozen others.*

For a second, she thought she heard Masson's voice. It was coming from a great distance, barely audible over the noise of torture, concrete and metal. Now there were two voices, and she realized they were close by, on the other side of the steel door.

"No!" she shouted, furious with herself for putting colleagues in danger. "Get away! Keep back"

Her words were drowned by a noise like an avalanche. The floor in the center of the room erupted in a shower of dirt, sending fragments of concrete and the two chairs flying.

Jo curled up, arms over her head, as debris rained around them. Then she stood up, choking on concrete dust, to confront the Follower. Its earth-body was vast, black as rich English soil, and trailing roots and fragments of copper cables. Faceless, it still sensed its prey somehow and turned towards Jo. In the cramped space, it couldn't stand upright, but instead loped like a gorilla out of the pit it had created.

"Goodbye Dylan," she said. "Wish I could say it's been nice knowing you."

The last thing she remembered was driving the taser into the vast, featureless head before an avalanche of cold earth overwhelmed her.

***

The door came loose just as Masson and Lewis shoulder-charged it. The steel slab fell inwards onto a mound of wet dirt and broken concrete. They shone their flashlights around the wrecked chamber. In a far corner, Masson glimpsed a colossal, man-like form. In the split-second it took to flick the beam back whatever had been there had collapsed into a heap of earth.

"Come on, we can still save her!" said Masson, clambering over to the black mound. He saw what he had thought to be a fragment of debris was an arm sticking out of the heaped soil. Between them, they dug out Jo with their hands and tried to resuscitate her with CPR. After half a minute, she was still not breathing. Then Lewis took the defibrillator from the medical kit and shocked her. The first jolt apparently did nothing.

"Keep trying! I can't lose her, not now!" cried Masson.

Miranda Bell was technically dead, but they saved her, he thought. *And she was in a much worse condition than Jo. That thing, whatever it is, left the job undone before ...*

"That's very touching, sir," murmured Jo, opening her eyes. "It feels good to be appreciated."

She sat up, eyes not quite focused, but still able to give a wan smile.

"Thanks, guys, but you shouldn't have risked it," she said.

"Where's Morgan?" asked Lewis.

Jo looked round and gestured at what looked like a half-buried heap of old clothes.

Lewis scrambled over to the crumpled body, shifted a chunk of concrete, and revealed what remained of Dylan Morgan's head.

"Collateral damage," said Masson. "The bastard wasn't as lucky as June Bell."

"But what happened?" asked Lewis. "What did this?"

"Don't name it, Jo!" shouted Masson, before he could help himself.

"Name what?" she asked. "Morgan overpowered me after I'd arrested him on suspicion of murder and brought me here. After that, things get rather hazy."

"And I have a feeling that's how they'll stay," said Masson. "Get it, Lewis?"

"Yes, boss."

"Good. Now," Masson continued, "let's get Jo out of here before the whole bloody place collapses."

***

That night a nurse came into Jo Garland's hospital room and found her patient staring at a small slip of paper.

"What's that?" asked the nurse. "Piece of evidence?"

"I doubt it," replied Jo. Then a thought struck her and she asked the nurse, "Can you see anything written on this?"

The young woman bent down over the bed and stared as Jo turned it over to show both sides. It was completely blank.

"No," the nurse said, "There's nothing on it. Why?"

Jo shook her head.

"Not sure," she admitted. "But I hope it means I'm off the hook. At least for now."

Epilogue

Mark stood on the terrace of the Grey Horse, looking out over the causeway. The tide was out and the way to the mainland was clear. In the June sunlight, the sea sparkled, gold sprayed on blue.

"Penny for your thoughts?" said Victor.

"Doctor Paterson says I should go to the nearest hospital for a proper check-up," said Mark.

"Always a good idea with a head injury."

Mark turned to look at the older man.

"You think I should chance it, then?"

Victor shrugged.

"The sensible, everyday part of me says of course you should. But after all we've seen ..."

Lucy appeared, collecting glasses. Mark had been surprised to find her carrying on with her regular life on the island. But, as she had pointed out, normal life always goes on, even in the strangest circumstances.

"Looks innocent enough," she remarked, as she paused at a nearby table. "But I don't think I'll be crossing any time soon."

When neither of the men replied, she said, "Look, I thought I was helping. I'm sorry it seemed to make things worse."

DO NOT LEAVE

That had been the only message received during their Ouija board session yesterday. Had it meant that Mark shouldn't leave Skara Farne? That none of the three participants should leave? Or that nobody at all should leave the island? They had discussed it, at first in bafflement, then in baffled rage. They had tried to re-establish contact with the messenger that claimed to be Summerskill, but to no avail. Now they waited, and wondered.

"The only conclusion I can reach, young man," said Victor, going to rejoin his pint, "is that you have a destiny."

Mark laughed.

"To get people killed?"

"You had no choice," said Lucy, putting a hand on his shoulder. "And she chose her path. She was courageous, a warrior if you like."

"I could have said no!"

"Tell yourself it was the concussion, then," offered Victor. "You weren't thinking straight."

But Mark didn't respond. He was looking instead at a figure standing at the end of the causeway. He had the distinct impression that the person was looking back at him, but it was hard to tell. The stranger was wearing an old-fashioned monk's garment, with a hood concealing his face.

* * *

FREE Bonus Novel!

Wow, I hope you enjoyed this book as much as I did writing it! If you enjoyed the book, please leave a review. Your reviews inspire me to continue writing about the world of spooky and untold horrors!

To really show you my appreciation for purchasing this book, please enjoy a **FREE extra spooky bonus novel.** This will surely leave you running scared!

Visit below to download your bonus novel and to learn about my upcoming releases, future discounts and giveaways: www.ScareStreet.com

FREE books (30 - 60 pages):
Ron Ripley (Ghost Stories)
1. Ghost Stories (Short Story Collection)
   www.scarestreet.com/ghost

A.I. Nasser (Supernatural Suspense)
2. Polly's Haven (Short Story)
   www.scarestreet.com/pollys
3. This is Gonna Hurt (Short Story)
   www.scarestreet.com/thisisgonna

Multi-Author Scare Street Collaboration
4. Horror Stories: A Short Story Collection
   www.scarestreet.com/horror

And experience the full-length novels (150 – 210 pages):
Ron Ripley (Ghost Stories)
1. Sherman's Library Trilogy (FREE via mailing list signup)
   www.scarestreet.com
2. The Boylan House Trilogy
   www.scarestreet.com/boylantri
3. The Blood Contract Trilogy
   www.scarestreet.com/bloodtri

4. The Enfield Horror Trilogy
www.scarestreet.com/enfieldtri

Moving In Series

5. **Moving In Series Box Set Books 1 - 3 (22% off)**
www.scarestreet.com/movinginbox123
6. Moving In (Book 1)
www.scarestreet.com/movingin
7. The Dunewalkers (Moving In Series Book 2)
www.scarestreet.com/dunewalkers
8. Middlebury Sanitarium (Book 3)
www.scarestreet.com/middlebury
9. **Moving In Series Box Set Books 4 - 6 (25% off)**
www.scarestreet.com/movinginbox456
10. The First Church (Book 4)
www.scarestreet.com/firstchurch
11. The Paupers' Crypt (Book 5)
www.scarestreet.com/paupers
12. The Academy (Book 6)
www.scarestreet.com/academy

Berkley Street Series

13. Berkley Street (Book 1)
www.scarestreet.com/berkley
14. The Lighthouse (Book 2)
www.scarestreet.com/lighthouse
15. The Town of Griswold (Book 3)
www.scarestreet.com/griswold
16. Sanford Hospital (Book 4)
www.scarestreet.com/sanford
17. Kurkow Prison (Book 5)
www.scarestreet.com/kurkow
18. Lake Nutaq (Book 6)
www.scarestreet.com/nutaq
19. Slater Mill (Book 7)
www.scarestreet.com/slater
20. Borgin Keep (Book 8)
www.scarestreet.com/borgin
21. Amherst Burial Ground (Book 9)
www.scarestreet.com/amherst

Hungry Ghosts Street Series

22. Hungry Ghosts (Book 1)
www.scarestreet.com/hungry

Haunted Collection Series
23. Collecting Death (Book 1)
www.scarestreet.com/collecting
24. Walter's Rifle (Book 2)
www.scarestreet.com/walter
25. Blood in the Mirror (Book 3)
www.scarestreet.com/bloodmirror

Victor Dark (Supernatural Suspense)
26. Uninvited Guests Trilogy
www.scarestreet.com/uninvitedtri
27. Listen To Me Speak Trilogy
www.scarestreet.com/listentri

A.I. Nasser (Supernatural Suspense)
Slaughter Series
28. Children To The Slaughter (Book 1)
www.scarestreet.com/children
29. Shadow's Embrace (Book 2)
www.scarestreet.com/shadows
30. Copper's Keeper (Book 3)
www.scarestreet.com/coppers
The Sin Series
31. Kurtain Motel (Book 1)
www.scarestreet.com/kurtain
32. Refuge (Book 2)
www.scarestreet.com/refuge
33. Purgatory (Book 3)
www.scarestreet.com/purgatory
The Carnival Series
34. Blood Carousel(Book 1)
www.scarestreet.com/bloodcarousel
Witching Hour Series
35. Witching Hour (Book 1)
www.scarestreet.com/witchinghour
36. Devil's Child (Book 2)
www.scarestreet.com/devilschild

David Longhorn (Supernatural Suspense)
The Sentinels Series
37. Sentinels (Book 1)
    www.scarestreet.com/sentinels
38. The Haunter (Book 2)
    www.scarestreet.com/haunter
39. The Smog (Book 3)
    www.scarestreet.com/smog
Dark Isle Series
40. Dark Isle (Book 1)
    www.scarestreet.com/darkisle
41. White Tower (Book 2)
    www.scarestreet.com/whitetower
42. The Red Chapel (Book 3)
    www.scarestreet.com/redchapel
Ouroboros Series
43. The Sign of Ouroboros (Book 1)
    www.scarestreet.com/ouroboros
44. Fortress of Ghosts (Book 2)
    www.scarestreet.com/fortress
45. Day of The Serpent (Book 3)
    www.scarestreet.com/serpent
Curse of Weyrmouth Series
46. Curse of Weyrmouth (Book 1)
    www.scarestreet.com/weyrmouth
47. Blood of Angels (Book 2)
    www.scarestreet.com/bloodofangels

Eric Whittle (Psychological Horror)
Catharsis Series
48. Catharsis (Book 1)
    www.scarestreet.com/catharsis
49. Mania (Book 2)
    www.scarestreet.com/mania
50. Coffer (Book 3)
    www.scarestreet.com/coffer
Sara Clancy (Supernatural Suspense)
Dark Legacy Series

51. Black Bayou (Book 1)
www.scarestreet.com/bayou
52. Haunted Waterways (Book 2)
www.scarestreet.com/waterways
53. Demon's Tide (Book 3)
www.scarestreet.com/demonstide

Banshee Series

54. Midnight Screams (Book 1)
www.scarestreet.com/midnight
55. Whispering Graves (Book 2)
www.scarestreet.com/whispering
56. Shattered Dreams (Book 3)
www.scarestreet.com/shattered

Black Eyed Children Series

57. Black Eyed Children (Book 1)
www.scarestreet.com/blackeyed
58. Devil's Rise (Book 2)
www.scarestreet.com/rise
59. The Third Knock (Book 3)
www.scarestreet.com/thirdknock

Demonic Games Series

60. Demonic Games (Book 1)
www.scarestreet.com/nesting
61. Buried (Book 2)
www.scarestreet.com/buried

Chelsey Dagner (Supernatural Suspense)
Ghost Mirror Series

62. Ghost Mirror (Book 1)
www.scarestreet.com/ghostmirror
63. The Gatekeeper (Book 2)
www.scarestreet.com/gatekeeper

Keeping it spooky,
Team Scare Street

13644599R00087

Printed in Great Britain
by Amazon